Anybody's Hero
The Battle of Old Men and Young Boys

By
Phyllis Hall Haislip

2013

For Kevin —

Enjoy!

Phyllis Hall Haislip

W̅M̅™ **WHITE MANE KIDS**
K̅IDS̅ SHIPPENSBURG, PENNSYLVANIA
15

This White Mane Books publication
was printed by
Beidel Printing House, Inc.
63 West Burd Street
Shippensburg, PA 17257-0708 USA

The acid-free paper used in this book meets the guidelines for
permanence and durability of the Committee on Production Guidelines for Book Longevity of the Council on Library Resources.

For a complete list of available publications
please write
White Mane Books
Division of White Mane Publishing Company, Inc.
P.O. Box 708
Shippensburg, PA 17257-0708 USA

Library of Congress Cataloging-in-Publication Data

Haislip, Phyllis Hall.
  Anybody's hero : the Battle of Old Men and Young Boys / by Phyllis Hall Haislip.
     p. cm. -- (White Mane kids ; 15)
  Summary: In June 1864, twelve-year-old Luca and his friend Jim join Luca's grandfather
and the other old men and boys of Petersburg, Virginia, to defend the city from the
advancing Union army.
  Includes bibliographical references (p.).
  ISBN 1-57249-343-7 (alk. paper)
  1. Petersburg (Va.)--History--Siege, 1864-1865--Juvenile fiction. [1. Petersburg
(Va.)--History--Siege, 1864-1865--Fiction. 2. Friendship--Fiction. 3.
Grandfathers--Fiction. 4. Virginia--History--Civil War, 1861-1865--Fiction. 5. United
States--History--Civil War, 1861-1865--Fiction.] I. Title. II. WM kids; 15.

PZ7.H128173An 2003
[Fic]--dc22

2003057630

For Otis
who knows why

Contents

Acknowledgments

Many people contributed to the making of this book: writers, librarians, museum professionals, editors, and computer experts. I would like to thank fellow writer, Mary Louise Clifford, who first read the manuscript and offered criticism and suggestions. I have appreciated the ongoing support of writer Sara Piccini. As always, the encouragement of Agnes King was invaluable.

The librarians and staff of the Williamsburg Regional Library have cheerfully and skillfully answered many queries, obtained books for me through interlibrary loan, and offered me support throughout the writing process.

I am especially grateful to the museum professionals who have offered their assistance. Chris Calkins of the Petersburg National Battlefield gave generously of his time and introduced me to a number of historical resources. He showed me the route of the battle and took me to key sites in the story. Laura Willoughby, curator of the Museums of the City of Petersburg, generously allowed me to photograph the doll "Pat" and other items in the collection. Michael Moore, curator of the Lee Hall Mansion, was helpful in tracking down Miss Maizie's clock. John Quarstein, Director, and G. Richard Hoffeditz, Jr., Curator, of the Virginia War Museum made it possible for me to photograph the museum's Mississippi rifle.

I want to thank all my editors. My son, Alexander Haislip, spent many hours editing the manuscript, bringing to it his writing expertise and the perspective of another generation. My husband, Otis Haislip, has also carefully read the manuscript for errors in content and grammatical problems. Special thanks to Marianne Zinn and Vicki Stouffer of the White Mane Editorial Department and to Nicole Riley, White Mane Publicity Director. Your diligent efforts are much appreciated.

Special thanks too go to Otis and Alex for technical assistance on the manuscript. They are always able to sort out the computer glitches that accompany a project such as this.

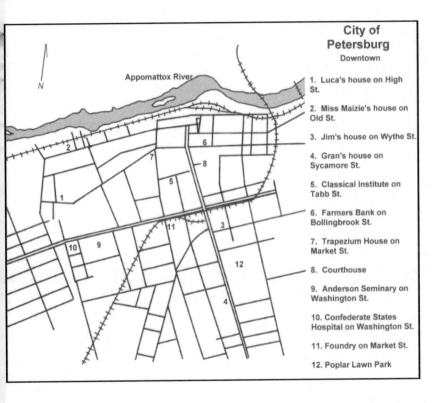

City of Petersburg
Downtown

1. Luca's house on High St.
2. Miss Maizie's house on Old St.
3. Jim's house on Wythe St.
4. Gran's house on Sycamore St.
5. Classical Institute on Tabb St.
6. Farmers Bank on Bollingbrook St.
7. Trapezium House on Market St.
8. Courthouse
9. Anderson Seminary on Washington St.
10. Confederate States Hospital on Washington St.
11. Foundry on Market St.
12. Poplar Lawn Park

Courtesy of Otis L. Haislip, Jr.

Luca's world centered around downtown Petersburg. This prosperous city was the second largest in Virginia during the Civil War and an important railroad and commercial center. The Dimmock Line stretched in a semi-circle of breastworks and batteries around the city.

Chapter 1

No Way for a Gentleman to Behave

"Bluebelly! Yankee! Spy!" Luca heard yells close behind him. He walked faster along East Bank Street. "Italian! Yankee! Dummy!" came another voice.

Luca turned to see Freddie Purdy, a big, red-haired boy, and his shadow, an anemic-looking, cross-eyed boy called Creepy Eddie. Both boys went to Anderson Seminary, a school for poor boys. Luca had noticed that whenever they could, these two bullies tormented boys from his school, Petersburg Classical Institute. He guessed they were jealous of the well-to-do boys that went to Classical.

Luca put his head down and kept walking. He hated being picked on. How dare they call him a Yankee spy! With the war between the Confederacy and the Northern states in its third year, and the invading Union army threatening even the Confederate capital at Richmond, it was about the worst thing they could call him. They were hateful. He passed Farmers Bank and crossed to the other side of the street. "Hey, you," yelled Freddie, "slow down if you're not a Yankee-Italian-Bluebelly!"

1

Farmers Bank

Author's Photograph

Luca's heart started to pound. He wanted to run. Instead, he slowed his pace and turned. A couple of small boys playing marbles in the street stopped to watch.

Luca said nothing. He pushed his unruly, dark hair off his damp forehead. He was just about out of patience. Today had not been a good day. After school, he had walked to the Adams farm on the outskirts of town to get fresh eggs for his mother. He usually didn't mind the chore, but today he had followed a group of boys from Classical for a good part of the way. They had not asked him to join them, and he had felt left out, excluded as if he really were a Yankee spy. He had tried to make friends in the two months since he and his mother moved to Petersburg. But the boys in Classical didn't seem to want anything to do with him, and these boys from Anderson were downright mean. He'd show them. He'd show them all.

Luca reached into his book bag and took out an egg. He pitched it right at Freddie Purdy. It hit the side of Freddie's stringy, red hair. The marble players laughed. Freddie's broad face flushed and with his right hand he swiped at the egg dripping down his neck. Without hesitating, Luca grabbed a second egg and hurled it at Creepy Eddie. The egg fell wide of its mark, and Luca reached into his bag again. He lobbed another egg at Eddie. It smashed into the boy's back as he fled up an alley between two brick office buildings.

Now Freddie Purdy's face was beet-red, his fingers were sticky with egg, and he was shouting, "I'll get even with you, you low-down foreigner!"

Luca groped for another egg and arced it at Freddie. Freddie jumped backward and it missed him, but he stumbled and almost fell. "You'll be sorry, you dirty Yankee," he yelled as he ran away. "I'll get you!"

Luca smiled at the retreating, egg-splattered bullies. This wasn't the first time they had taunted him. He felt fine for a few moments, thinking about the mess in Purdy's hair. Then he realized that he had only two eggs left and no money to buy more. The War of Secession had caused Confederate money to lose its value and eggs were expensive. He had made the long hike to the Adams farm for the eggs, and now he would have to go home without them. What would his mother say? She needed the eggs for a cake, and she didn't approve of fighting.

Luca didn't share his mother's views on fighting. Ever since he had gotten his first toy soldiers, he had imagined taking part in heroic adventures. Someday, he would be a hero.

Right now, however, the prospect of telling his mother what had happened filled him with dread. He knew she wouldn't punish him, but her look of disappointment would be worse than any punishment. His elation at pelting Freddie and Creepy Eddie with the eggs passed as Luca thought of his mother and Freddie's parting threat. What would happen the next time he crossed paths with Freddie Purdy?

Luca headed toward home, trying to decide what he would tell his mother. He walked about half a block when someone called after him in a commanding tone. "Boy!"

Luca recognized the deep voice. He turned. His grandfather stood, wide-brimmed hat in hand, scowling at him. He was an old man, at least sixty, with a shock of white hair and a full beard, as bristly as his abrupt manner. Before moving to Petersburg from Richmond, Luca had seen his grandfather only six or seven times. Luca's father was a diplomat, and he was far away in England, trying to secure aid for the Confederate government. Before leaving, his father had helped Luca and his Italian mother move to Petersburg where they would be closer to family. But so far, Luca's Virginian relatives hadn't been especially friendly. His fair-skinned aunts and blue-eyed cousins seemed uneasy around them, and they insisted on calling him Luke, the English version of his name. Their confusion was understandable since he'd been named for his grandfather. Yet, he didn't like to be called Luke, instead of Luca. His grandfather was even worse. He was always gruff and never called him anything but "boy."

"Boy," the senior Luke Streetman said again. His heavy eyebrows knitted into a frown.

Luca went to where his grandfather stood in front of Farmers Bank.

"Dad blame it! I saw you just now," his grandfather said. He raised his hand and pointed a finger at Luca. "That's no way for a gentleman to behave."

"No, sir," said Luca, looking his grandfather directly in the eyes. His father had told him again and again that he should always look people in the eyes.

"Saturday morning. Ten o'clock. Meet me at the woodshed behind the house."

"Yes, sir," Luca said, realizing that he was being dismissed. He again headed toward home. He had read or heard that the woodshed was the place where boys in the South were punished. He felt like Atlas, carrying the world on his shoulders. Why did they ever come here? Petersburg was an awful place.

"Boy!" his grandfather called after him.

What now? Luca thought. He took a deep breath and went to where the old man stood with a hand in the pocket of his well-tailored suit. His grandfather took out a wad of Confederate dollars and gave him several. "Get some eggs at McIlwaine's. This is between us. Understand?"

"Yes, sir," Luca said as he took the dollars. "Thank you, sir."

Luca didn't like the idea of keeping something from his mother, but he didn't want to tell her about the eggs or the fighting. In any case, his grandfather was not the kind of person you contradicted. Luca headed for McIlwaine's store, wondering what the old man had in mind for him on Saturday. As soon as he rounded the corner, Luca took one of the last two eggs from his book bag and flung it furiously at a white picket fence he was passing. It exploded with a satisfying splat.

A. G. McILWAINE.   R. D. McILWAINE.

McILWAINE, SON & CO.

WHOLESALE GROCERS

AND

COMMISSION MERCHANTS,

Nos. 79, 81, 83, 85 Sycamore Street,

PETERSBURG, VA.

Keep constantly on hand a large and well selected stock of Groceries, Guano and other Fertilizers. Liberal Advances on Produce consigned to them. Particular attention to Sales.

An advertisement for McIlwaine's Grocery Store

Eugene Ferslew, *Directory for the City of Petersburg for 1860.*
Petersburg: George E. Ford

Chapter 2

A Piece of Brick

"Streetman, how would you translate the next sentence?" Luca's teacher asked the next morning in class. Luca sat up straight and brushed his hair back. He sighed. It was hot in the classroom. May sunshine streamed through the high windows, and he had been watching a lethargic fly repeatedly hit the glass with a dull thud. He couldn't concentrate on class. All he could think about was the upcoming meeting with his grandfather. He looked at Mr. Barnum, a gaunt, middle-aged man, who was pursing his thin lips and glaring at him. The teacher was so thin and pale that the students called him Cadaver Barnum. Luca stared down at his Latin book. He'd lost the place.

"Pay attention," said the teacher. "*Castrum nostrum...*"

Luca put his finger under the sentences, scowled for a moment, and then translated the Latin. "Our camp...," he began. He paused. Latin was easy for Luca. It was similar to the Italian of Venice, Italy, where he had spent the first seven years of his life. And last year at his school in Richmond, his class had worked all the way through

Petersburg Classical Institute
Courtesy of the Petersburg Museums, City of Petersburg

Caesar's *Gallic Wars*. He knew, however, that if he appeared too smart, he'd never make any friends.

The vein on Mr. Barnum's neck stood out. "Go on, Streetman," he said, his voice betraying his annoyance.

"Our camp sat on the... *fiume*," Luca blurted out.

The other boys broke into fits of laughter. Sometimes when he was under pressure, the English word didn't come to him and Luca said the Italian word instead. For some reason, his classmates seemed to find Luca's mistakes hilarious. He felt his face grow red.

"No, no, Streetman," said Mr. Barnum, shaking his skeletal head. "Quiet everyone!" He was clearly exasperated since he knew from the principal at Luca's school last year that the boy was an outstanding Latin student. "Prentice," the teacher turned to a thin, sensitive-looking boy who sat near the front of the room.

"Our camp sat near the river," said Jim Prentice with a sympathetic glance at Luca.

The clock on the courthouse began to bong. It was noon and before the clock finished striking, Mr. Barnum stood up and said, "Class dismissed." The boys watched the teacher leave the room and then leapt from their seats.

Luca took a moment to pack up his books. He glanced up to see Jim Prentice walk out of the classroom with his Latin book balanced on his head. Luca shook his head. Jim Prentice was strange.

Jake Leighton and Ben McIlwaine stood in the doorway. Jake was a blond, good-looking boy who was the leader of the boys Luca had seen yesterday on his way to get eggs, and easy-going, athletic Ben was always at Jake's side. Jake and Ben had formed a club, and Luca was convinced they were up to something interesting. He hoped that he would be asked to join their group.

"We heard you served Freddie and Eddie scrambled eggs," said Jake.

"You could say that," said Luca, hoping that the incident had won him the admiration of the boys.

"Purdy called you a Bluebelly and a Yankee spy," said Jake. "Of course, we don't believe it. It's ridiculous."

Luca wasn't sure he liked the tone of this remark. These boys had not been friendly to him, but they had not been openly hostile like Freddie Purdy and Creepy Eddie. Luca knew Jake and Ben had been watching him, trying to make up their minds about him. Perhaps this was some kind of test. He must be careful how he handled himself. "Eddie and Freddie must have heard that we lived in New York for two years before the war started. I guess they didn't bother to hear anything else," said Luca.

"We've heard your mother does her own gardening. Is that true?" asked Ben. He wrinkled his nose as if he smelled soured milk.

Luca was surprised at the turn the conversation had taken. He thought Ben's question was stupid. But he knew from experience that people were curious about foreigners. "My mother likes to garden," he said.

"But your mother might perspire," said Ben.

"Ladies in Petersburg don't do their own work, and they especially don't do slave work," Jake said.

Luca didn't know how to reply. He guessed they already had heard about his mother's views on slavery. "My mother doesn't hold with slavery," he said. "We have two free blacks who work for us. We pay Ree to clean and Jordan to help with the garden."

"So the rumors are true. No wonder Freddie and Eddie called you a Yankee and a spy," Jake said. He smiled and nudged Ben as if this was some kind of joke.

Luca pushed aside the lock of hair that was forever falling onto his forehead and tried to stay calm. He resented their comments, but he hoped that once he had explained everything, it would clear the air. "My father is an aide to President Davis. When the war started, he brought my mother and me to Virginia. Right now he's in London, working for the Confederate cause. Lots of people in Petersburg don't believe in slavery. My father told me the city first voted to support the Union. You know so much about Petersburg and what's going on with my family, surely you must know all this."

"Of course, everybody in Petersburg knows the Streetmans," said Ben.

Luca sensed that Ben was backing off a little. Jake, however, wasn't about to stop badgering Luca. "Your father married a foreigner, and he worked in New York City. I can see where some people hereabouts might think he's become a Yankee," he said. His voice was neutral, but Luca's jaw tightened.

"How dare you suggest such a thing," Luca said, raising his voice. He was trying not to be riled, but there were limits.

At that moment, Cadaver Barnum appeared in the hallway beyond the door. He had apparently forgotten something in the classroom. Jake and Ben moved into the corridor and went out the front door. Luca swallowed his growing rage and followed them.

"One minute, young man," said his teacher.

Luca stopped and turned. "Yes, sir."

"What's all this nonsense in Latin class? I know you are proficient in Latin. Are you playing games with me, Streetman?"

"No sir," said Luca, thinking quickly. "I wasn't paying attention. I was sleeping with my eyes open."

"Sleeping with your eyes open?" the teacher said in a peevish voice. "I've always suspected that some students have that ability. But you're the first student to admit it."

"I'm quite good at it, sir," said Luca, forcing a lopsided smile.

"Well, see that you don't do it again," Mr. Barnum said with a wave of his bony hand. "You may go now."

Luca looked for Jake and Ben as he left school, but they were not outside. Luca headed home. The day was fine, and it was good to be out of class, but he was still angry. How dare anyone suggest that his father was a Yankee when he was doing important work for the Confederate government! The boys in this town were rotten. And his grandfather, what did he have in mind? Why had he been so gruff? Why wasn't he friendlier?

Luca neared the corner where he turned on High Street. Two boys were standing on the street corner. They were intently studying something in the grass. Both had their eyes on the ground. One boy poked at something with a stick. It was Freddie Purdy and Creepy Eddie.

Luca wasn't sure they had seen him. To avoid them, he'd have to go out of his way to get home. He didn't know the city very well yet. But he quickly crossed to the other side of the street. A heavily loaded freight wagon was slowly making its way down Market Street toward the river. He paced himself and made sure he stayed behind it until he got to Old Street. From there, he knew he could circle back to his house on High Street.

Luca was angry as he headed up Old Street. He was already late for lunch. Now he had to go a long way around to get home. He kicked a piece of brick that had come loose from the brick sidewalk. It didn't go very far. So he kicked it harder. This time the brick sped forward until, wham, it hit the steps of the house he was passing. The house, built in the early years of the century, was right on the street. The brick bounced up and whacked the front door before rolling off the porch with a clatter. It came to rest in the small flowerbed beside the porch.

"I've done it now," Luca said as he saw the door begin to open.

Chapter 3

Crazy Maizie

A huge man as black as the inside of a cookstove stood in the doorway. He had fierce, hawklike eyes and a flattened nose. In spite of his ferocious appearance, he was neatly dressed in a well-tailored, black suit. He was the biggest man Luca had ever seen, except for the time long ago when he had gone to the circus. The man, standing as he did at the top of three steep steps that led up to the front door, looked like a giant from a fairy tale. "What do you want?" he asked. His question was polite, but his manner was guarded.

"Well," Luca began, trying to think what he should say, "I didn't actually knock on the door."

The big man frowned. "Are you playing jokes on Eli and Miss Maizie?" His tone was threatening.

"No, sir," said Luca, "I can explain."

Just then a small, bent, white-haired lady in an old-fashioned cap came to the door. "Who has come to see my Pat?" she asked.

"My name is Luca Streetman," Luca answered, beginning to worry where this all might be leading.

"Streetman," the woman said, looking a bit confused, "why, I've known Luke Streetman all my life, and you're not him."

"No, madam," Luca said, "I'm his grandson. I was named for him."

"Oh, how nice," the woman said. Her face brightened. "Luke's grandson has come to see Pat. Come right in, young man. Eli, please tell Sara to make tea."

"Yes, ma'am," said Eli. The big man retreated from the doorway with a resigned look.

Luca had no choice. He had been taught manners, and good manners dictated that he respect his elders. He followed the old lady inside.

"I've heard about you," the old woman said. "Your father, Lawrence, is a diplomat in London. Your mother is Italian."

"Yes, ma'am," said Luca. The old lady led him into a sitting room. It was a bright, sun-filled room crowded with highly polished Chippendale furniture that had gone out of style decades before. A battle-scarred, old, black cat was curled up on the window seat. The cat yawned and looked sleepily at Luca before stretching and settling back down on the cushion.

"I'm Mrs. Maizie Thornton. You may sit in my dear, deceased husband's chair," she said, indicating a blue, damask-covered wing chair near the fireplace. "Your father or grandfather has probably told you about my Pat."

Luca's father had not told him about Pat, but in the short time he had been in Petersburg, he had heard the other children talk about Crazy Maizie. He hadn't paid much attention to what they said. Now he wished he had listened more carefully. He didn't know what to say, but the old woman kept on chattering.

"We'll have tea. Then you can see Pat," Miss Maizie said.

Luca began to protest. "It's lunchtime, ma'am, and my mother is expecting me home."

"We'll have tea and then you can see Pat," the old woman persisted. "And you must promise me you will bring your mother to visit soon. No visit to Petersburg is complete without seeing Pat."

"We're not exactly visiting Petersburg." Luca explained to her how they had happened to come to Petersburg.

"Are you living with your grandparents?"

"They offered to put us up, but their house is full. My two aunts and my cousins are staying there," said Luca. "We're renting the Ingram house on High Street. We looked for a place for months. Then we learned that the Ingrams had decided to go to the country to keep an eye on their farm. So we're renting their house. We were lucky to find it with all the refugees in town."

"I heard the Ingrams had left town," Miss Maizie said, frowning a little. "So many people coming and going these days. It's hard to get used to. But you must promise me that you'll bring your mother by to see Pat."

"Yes, ma'am," Luca said, trying to hide his growing exasperation, "I'll bring my mother to visit soon."

"Someday next week," said Miss Maizie. "I'll send Eli with a note."

"That will be fine," Luca said, wondering what he had gotten them into.

"I bet you didn't know that people have come all the way from Richmond to see my Pat."

"No, ma'am."

"And since people like your father travel all over the world, I expect Pat is known in more places than I could ever guess." Just then, the maid came in with a tray. She was a heavy woman with big, protruding eyes. "Thank you, Sara," Miss Maizie said. "Just put it on the table."

Luca eyed the dish of fancy tea cakes and his stomach growled. His mother would be waiting lunch for him. How would he ever explain what had happened? He sat patiently while Miss Maizie poured tea into bone-china cups as fragile as the old lady herself. Then she fixed him a little plate of cakes. While she rambled on, he tried to figure out what he would tell his mother.

Luca glanced at the wall clock. Below the clock's face was a painted picture of Venice, the city where he had been born. He wished he was there now. The minutes were going by slowly, but it was already 12:30, and he had to be back in class at one. He wanted to ask Miss Maizie about the clock, but he was afraid that would prolong his visit. So, he just sat there, listening to her talk. Finally, Miss

Clock with Venetian canal scene below the face

Courtesy of Lee Hall Mansion

Maizie put down her cup and got up. "I know you're anxious to see Pat. I won't keep you waiting any longer."

Luca jumped up, almost upsetting the tea table. Miss Maizie didn't seem to notice, or if she did, she didn't say anything.

"Follow me, young man." Miss Maizie led him into the next room. It was a formal parlor, and like the sitting room, it was full of old-fashioned furniture. Miss Maizie walked to a small chair. "Here's my Pat."

Luca stared at the doll that sat there. She was about eighteen inches tall and wore a plaid gingham dress like little girls wore long ago. She was made of cloth and ordinary looking, except that she had no face.

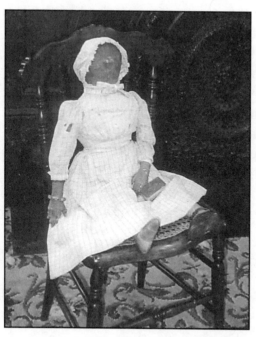

Pat
Courtesy of the Petersburg Museums,
City of Petersburg

Chapter 4

Pat

"Pat belonged to my cousin Jane. She knew I always wanted to own Pat. So she gave her to me. That was many years ago," said Miss Maizie.

"Why doesn't she have a face?" Luca asked.

"I don't really know. A friend of the family made the doll for Jane. I wish now I'd asked Jane more about Pat. But since Jane's been dead for years, I'll probably never know. There's a little poem that goes with Pat, and it says she will wear many faces: 'Adversity may frown on thee, But still serene, and calm you'll be...'"

Luca thought dolls were dumb. This doll was interesting though, even if she was strange looking. "She's very nice," he managed to say.

"I've always had a special place in my heart for Pat. Imagine going through the years with no face. Poor thing. How awful for her."

"I really must go now," said Luca. "My mother will think I've been eaten by an...*ottopode.*" His face reddened. He had done it again, blurted out something stupid. This time he had said the Italian word for octopus.

"She mustn't think that," said Miss Maizie with serious concern as if she understood what he had said. She reached up and pulled a faded, red-velvet cord. Eli appeared a moment later. "Please show young Master Streetman to the door."

"This way, sir," said Eli. The massive man led Luca to the front door and opened it. "You be careful in the future, young sir," Eli cautioned. His words were polite, but his piercing look made Luca realize that he was being warned. He bounded down the steps and ran toward High Street. He didn't slow until he neared the brick house with its fan doorway where he lived with his mother.

Luca's mother was standing at their gate. Her pretty, oval face was fixed in a frown. "I'm sorry, Madre," he gasped. "I'm all right, but I have to leave right away or I'll be late for school."

"No you don't, young man," his mother said in rapid Italian. "Inside and sit down. I'll write your teacher a note. After I've heard your explanation."

Luca went inside with his mother. The table was set for lunch. But she didn't offer him anything to eat.

Luca thought it best not to mention what Jake and Ben had said, but he told her about kicking the brick and about his visit with Crazy Maizie. "I'm sorry, Madre," he said again. "But I really couldn't get away, and I think you'll have to visit the old lady."

"It's about time somebody in this town invited me for tea." Madre had calmed down now and spoke in the British-sounding English she used with her son and husband most of the time.

She got up from the table and cut Luca two slices of bread and a piece of cheese. "And how was your morning in school?" she asked as she poured him a glass of milk.

"Nobody likes me. I'm tired of being called an Italian. Father thought that since he knew a lot of people here, I'd automatically have lots of friends."

"You'll make friends." Madre's voice was full of assurance. "And there are worse things than being called 'Italian.'" Luca knew that was true.

"Nobody has been very friendly toward you," he said.

"It's been a long time since your father lived in Petersburg. Your grandfather sent your father away to school after his mother died."

"Then grandfather married again and had a new family. I know that, but it wouldn't hurt my step-grandmother, Mrs. S., and all my aunts and cousins to be a little nicer." Luca hated feeling like an outsider. It had taken him a long time to make friends in Richmond and then they moved here. He longed to tell his mother about the incident with the eggs and his uneasiness over the coming meeting with his grandfather. But he kept quiet.

Madre shook her head. "I don't understand them," she said. "In Italy, family is family, no matter how distant the kinship. Perhaps we are oversensitive. They did invite us for Sunday dinner last week, and that's a start."

"I wish Father was in the Confederate army. It would be grand if he came to visit us in a gray uniform with a red sash. Maybe he would even wear a plume in his hat like General Jeb Stuart. I don't want him to get hurt, of course, but at least then I wouldn't always have to explain what he does. Being a diplomat isn't very heroic."

"I'm proud of your father, and you know how I feel about fighting." Luca heard the grandfather clock in the hall strike one. "You had better get back to class," his mother said, standing up.

Luca got up from the table and gave his mother a hug. *"Ciao,"* he said.

"One second," she said, writing a few lines on a piece of note paper, "here's your note, and be sure to come right home after school. I want you to help Jordan in the garden. I've had enough worry for one day."

Chapter 5

Pins and Packages

Luca was glad when school was finally over for the day. Outside, Jim Prentice was waiting for him.

"Would you like me to show you the fortifications?" Jim asked. He peered at Luca through thick glasses. "Since you're new in town, you probably haven't seen much of the Dimmock Line."

"No, I haven't seen the Dimmock Line, and I'd like to," said Luca, grateful that one of his classmates seemed interested in getting to know him, even if that person was the class brain. "But I'm supposed to help Jordan in the garden."

"I've heard your mother is planting a garden," said Jim with sincere interest.

"I guess it's all over town," said Luca, shaking his head. "When we lived in Richmond, our house barely had a yard. My mother was determined that in Petersburg we would have a garden. I don't understand why everyone is talking about it."

"*Ladies* in town would never dirty their hands in a garden, unless it's to cut a bouquet of flowers." Jim emphasized the word *ladies* in such a way that it was clear that he did not approve of the upper-class snob-bery in Petersburg.

Luca scowled. "My Italian grandfather owns acres and acres of vineyard on the mainland. He grows so many grapes, he can't possibly prune them all himself. Yet he tries, even though he's a busy man who owns a glass factory. I remember as a very little boy going by boat to the vineyard with him. I guess gardening is in my mother's bones and in mine too. When my mother knew we could rent the Ingram house, she wrote my grandfather in Italy and he sent her Italian seeds."

"I'd be curious to see what she grows. If I wasn't planning on becoming an engineer someday, I'd be-come an agronomist or a veterinarian. I'd experiment with plants or animals. I got a book from the library that tells about breeding horses." Jim seemed lost in thought for a moment. "It's a fascinating book." He held out the book and flipped the pages for Luca to see the illustrations.

"Very interesting," said Luca, not knowing how he was supposed to react to the drawings of pregnant horses.

"Anyway, what about seeing the defenses tomorrow?"

"That'll be good." Luca knew his mother would be happy to hear that he was making friends. She wouldn't know Jim Prentice was an outcast like himself.

Jim put the book on his head and walked away without even saying goodbye. Luca smiled. Jim was different. No question about it.

At home, Luca went to the kitchen. There he found Ree, their cleaning lady, washing the kitchen window. She was a pleasant, hardworking woman with skin as black as coffee grounds and no teeth. She must have found having no teeth embarrassing because she almost never smiled.

"Where's Madre?" asked Luca.

Ree polished the glass. "She's in the garden with Jordan," she said. She smiled at Luca with her mouth closed. "There's a plate of molasses cookies in the cupboard."

Luca thanked Ree and found the cookies. He went upstairs to change his school clothes before going to find his mother in the back yard.

"Luca, I'm glad you're home," his mother said, standing up from where she was separating seedlings. She wiped her hands on her apron. "You can rake where Jordan has spaded. It's time I started supper. Maybe I will be able to plant these later."

Luca picked up the rake and went to the corner where Jordan was working. He nodded at Jordan. "How are you today, Jordan?"

Jordan stopped spading for a moment. He was only sixteen, but with laborers scarce because of the war, Luca's mother had been lucky to find him to help in the garden. Jordan worked as a body servant and errand boy for Carter Wiley, the crippled son of former United States Congressman George Wiley. A wide smile brightened Jordan's dark face. "I'm as right as rain," he said. "I heard you visited Crazy Maizie today."

Luca's face fell. "I can't do anything without the whole town knowing about it. Don't people have anything better to do than keep track of my comings and goings?"

"Now don't get heated up. Miss Maizie's Sara is my aunt. And she's always telling us about Miss Maizie."

Jordan resumed his digging, and Luca began raking the grass out of the newly spaded earth. A few minutes later, Jordan asked, "Did you see Pat?"

"Doesn't everybody?" replied Luca, annoyed that he was the subject of gossip. He wondered if one of the town gossips would tell Madre about the eggs.

"You won't catch me looking at that Pat." Jordan stopped working again. "Aunt Sara told me that sometimes Miss Maizie just sits all alone with Pat. Aunt Sara says that she doesn't know what goes on in the parlor, but she has seen Miss Maizie in there with the pin box."

"The pin box?" Luca stopped raking.

"Aunt Sara says that Miss Maizie pretends she's sewing, but Aunt Sara says when no one is looking, the old lady sticks straight pins into Pat."

"Whatever for?"

"Aunt Sara says she puts the hex on people she doesn't like. She didn't get along with Mrs. Throwbridge, her neighbor. And the next thing we knew, Mrs. Throwbridge up and died. She wasn't even sick."

"How old was Mrs. Throwbridge?"

"About as old as Miss Maizie. They had been fighting for years over who owned the dogwood tree between their two houses. Truth is that it's gotten so big, it's on both lots."

"Couldn't Mrs. Throwbridge just have died?"

"Sure. But after that, for a long time Miss Maizie never went near Pat. Aunt Sara looked high and low for the pin box, and she never found it. She had to buy Miss Maizie new pins."

"Tell me about Eli. He's such a big fellow, how come he isn't out digging trenches and helping repair the fortifications?"

"He did work on the fortifications a while back, but Miss Maizie pulled strings and got him out of it," Jordan said.

That information peaked Luca's interest. "Are Eli and your Aunt Sara slaves or free? A lot of your people in Petersburg seem to be free."

"Eli's a slave. But he's never known his place. He's always been uppity. He acts like being Miss Maizie's butler, and fetching and carrying for her all the day long sets him above everybody else. My Aunt Sara's free," said Jordan. "My whole family's been free as long as anyone can remember, and Eli still looks down that big, old flat nose of his at Aunt Sara. He's too uppity for his own good."

"Eli seems to take care of Miss Maizie."

"He's just looking out for himself," Jordan said, scratching his head. "He collects the rents on her properties and looks after them, and..." He paused with the skill of a natural storyteller.

"Well? What else?"

"My Aunt Sara goes home at night. But she says sometimes Eli brings Miss Maizie packages."

"Packages of what?"

"Aunt Sara doesn't know. But she suspects that it's something for spells. You know—roosters' combs, bloodroot, stuff like that."

Luca didn't know exactly what Jordan meant. But Luca suspected from Jordan's tone that it was something evil. "What makes you think that is what's in the packages?"

"Because Eli visits Boadicea outside of town. She's the herb woman."

"Maybe Miss Maizie is getting something for her lumbago. Old folks always have some ailment or other."

"Boadicea's a witch," said Jordan with certainty. He picked up his shovel, signaling an end to the conversation.

Luca didn't know what to make of the things Jordan told him. He was becoming, like everyone else in Petersburg, curious about things that were none of his business. He stooped to shake red dirt off a thick clump of sod and resumed raking.

Chapter 6

The Hideout

"Let's leave our book bags on the porch of my aunt's house," Jim said the next afternoon when he met Luca after school. "It's not far from here."

"Nice house," said Luca as they deposited their bags and jackets on the wide porch that went all across the front of the big, white house.

Jim snorted. "Nice, if you're not a poor in-law."

"What do you mean?"

"I guess you haven't heard. I attend Petersburg Classical on scholarship. My mother, sister, and I live with my Aunt Mary Louise and Uncle Pete."

"Where's your father?"

"Killed at First Manassas."

"I'm sorry."

"He was in the Petersburg Grays. He was an engineer and cartographer. He made great maps of the Dimmock Line."

"I didn't mean to pry."

"That's okay. I've gotten used to my father being gone. It's been three years now. What I'm not used to is my mother." Jim's face was grave.

"What's the matter with her?"

"She took to bed after Father died. She just doesn't care anymore about Emmy and me." Jim sighed. "I think about her a lot. I don't know how to help."

Luca didn't know what to say. Surely what Jim said about his mother must not be true. Luca found it hard to imagine Madre not caring about him. They walked in silence. Finally, he asked, "How old is Emmy?"

"Emmy's twenty months younger than I am. She's eleven. She goes to Leavenworth Female Seminary. She's another charity scholar. By the way, Classical and Anderson are having a ball game tomorrow after school. Would you like to go with Emmy and me?"

"Sure," said Luca. He felt a wave of disappointment that there was going to be a baseball game and he hadn't been asked to play. He liked baseball. He had played in Richmond, and he had a pretty good throwing arm. Sometimes he had even pitched. "Is that why some of the guys in our class, Jake and Ben and their friends, were waiting around after school?"

"I suspect so."

"Since most of the boys will be at the ball field, there's someplace I'd like to go after we've seen the Confederate defenses."

"Where's that?"

"I'm not quite sure. But I can show you." Luca explained how he had seen Jake and the other boys hauling a railroad tie into the woods when he had followed them on his way to the Adams farm. "I'd like to see what they're up to. Today would be a good day since they seem to be staying at school to practice for the game tomorrow."

"I'll go along. Anything's better than going home."

Twenty minutes later they reached the Dimmock Line. "Amazing," Luca said, "I had no idea the defensive line was so long."

"It stretches for ten miles in a horseshoe around the city. You probably know," Jim said, "that these mounds of earth are called earthworks. The fifty-five artillery emplacements spaced at intervals are called batteries. The problem is that most of the batteries don't have guns." He explained how the Dimmock Line had been built early in the war and then neglected. He pointed out special features of the earthworks near where they stood.

Luca was impressed with Jim's knowledge of the technical aspects of the line. "Petersburg must be pretty important to have such extensive fortifications."

"Everyone says that Petersburg is essential to the Confederacy because of the railroads. I've heard that General Lee is prepared to defend the city at any cost."

"The town is full of soldiers, but sometimes I feel like there isn't a war going on at all. People just go about their business as usual."

"I don't think you'll be feeling that way for long. My uncle says a Yankee attack could come any time now. He's concerned because the fortifications need repair. The Dimmock Line was great when it was built, but it hasn't been maintained."

Luca climbed to the top of the earthwork and looked around, trying to get his bearings. "How do we get to the Adams house from here?" he asked.

"It's over there," said Jim, pointing to a house surrounded by trees.

Luca had never been in the Virginia woods, and as they neared the Adams house and the woods beyond it, he felt uneasy. "Are there any poisonous snakes hereabout?"

"A few rattlers. Copperheads. I've never seen one though."

"Do you go into the woods often?"

"Not very. I really don't have anybody to do anything with except Emmy. She loves the woods, but I'd rather be reading in the library."

Luca had mentally marked the place where he had seen the boys enter the woods. It was near a big holly tree, and he had no trouble finding the place. There was only the whisper of a trail, but they eagerly followed it. Luca led the way, and Jim tagged along behind.

"Look," Jim called out. Luca turned to see him pointing at a small, red-plumed bird high in a tree overhead.

"What is it?"

"A scarlet tanager. They're hard to spot. They like the deep woods. I've never seen one before."

"Do you know all the birds?"

"There are a few I haven't studied."

"Does it bother you that you're known as the class brain?"

"Not at all. I like to know things, and if people would rather be ignorant, that's their problem."

Luca thought about this for a moment. Jim had a point, but Luca was glad that no one in his class knew that he had been moved ahead a grade.

"Slow down a little," said Jim a moment later. Luca turned to see Jim studying a small white flower. "It's called a may apple. See, it looks like a little umbrella. It's not like an apple at all."

Just then, a twig snapped. Both boys stood still and listened, but they didn't hear anything else. The woods became thicker. Jim slapped at a mosquito, and Luca flinched when he heard the loud sound.

They came to a huge, fallen oak. Luca scrambled up on it to look around. "We've found it! Come on," he said, leaping down the other side of the tree.

"It's a trench and earthwork," said Jim as he followed Luca into the clearing. "It's just like the Dimmock Line."

"This really is something." Luca gave a low whistle of appreciation.

"Look, what I've found!" Jim was examining the earthwork.

The boys had dug a cave into the side of the earthwork. It wasn't very big, but it was shored up with two railroad ties. "They must have been working on this for months," said Luca.

"How did they do all this?"

"They must have shovels and other tools," said Luca. "They probably have stashed them somewhere close. What do you suppose they do here?"

"Play war for one thing. It's obviously their secret hideout. They have a club and this is their headquarters. If I had a place like this, I would come here all the time to be alone and think," Jim said. He pointed through the trees. "We're not far from the river. It's just over there. They may come here by boat sometimes. Do you want to take a look along the riverbank?"

"Next time," Luca said. "We better make ourselves scarce in case ball practice is over."

Luca and Jim made their way back to the road. "I now know why those guys aren't interested in the Dimmock Line. They have their own earthworks," Jim said, shaking his head. It was clear to Luca that Jim was revising his opinion of Jake, Ben, and the others.

Twenty minutes later they were back in town. "See you tomorrow," Jim said when they got to the corner of Luca's street. "Don't forget the ball game."

"I won't," said Luca. He was feeling low. The Saturday meeting with his grandfather was one day closer, and once he'd seen the boys' hideout in the woods, he'd known that they weren't likely to ask him to join their group. They'd done too much together making their secret place.

Chapter 7

The Ball Game

Luca spotted Jim and his sister as soon as he arrived at the ball field near Anderson Seminary the next afternoon. Jim had described Emmy only as liking the outdoors. Luca had imagined Emmy would look like Jim, only with long hair. He was glad to see that she didn't wear thick glasses and wasn't tall and paper-thin. She had long, brown braids, a turned-up nose, and a saucy smile.

"Hello," he said, holding out his hand to her, "I'm Luca. You must be Emmy."

Emmy took his hand. "Nice to meet you, Luca." She let go of his hand and then curtsied to him like a play actress. "Milord."

Not to be outdone, Luca pretended to take off a hat and presented her with a sweeping bow. "Charmed, Milady." They both laughed.

"If we go over there," Jim said, "we'll be able to see better."

They walked to the other side of the playing field. The day was sultry with dark clouds gathering to the west. The students who had come to watch the two

Anderson Seminary
Courtesy of the Petersburg Museums, City of Petersburg

rival schools play ball seemed to be in high spirits. It was Friday afternoon, and school was over for the week.

Luca had been feeling depressed all day. Tomorrow was Saturday, and Saturday was the day he was to meet his grandfather behind the woodshed. But meeting Emmy was like seeing the sun after days of rain.

"We have to cheer for Anderson," said Emmy with a toss of her head. "That's where the real people go to school. The boys from Classical are stuck up."

"Real people like Freddie Purdy and Creepy Eddie?" asked Luca, raising an eyebrow.

Emmy made a face. "I heard about the eggs. Good for you. Freddie's rotten. I saw him torture Miss Maizie's cat. He tried to hang it up by its tail. And he says dirty things to girls when no one is around. But some of the other Anderson boys are nice," she said. "At least they're not snobs like Jake Leighton and his crowd."

Luca looked for Freddie and Eddie among the Anderson ballplayers. He finally spotted them off to one side with some tough-looking Irish boys from across the tracks.

The game began. Luca watched enviously. Classical scored first and then Anderson tied the score. Luca was concentrating on the game, and yet, Emmy was determined to get to know all about him. She asked question after question. She was the first person since he had come to Petersburg who seemed curious at all about his life in Richmond, New York, and Italy. "Tell me more about Venice," she pleaded. "Did you go everywhere in a gondola?"

"There are some streets in Venice, so I walked to church, but I took a gondola to school."

"Do the gondoliers sing?"

"Fortunately, they don't sing on the way to school in the morning. Mostly, they sing for tourists."

One of the Anderson School boys was at bat and he hit a foul ball. It sailed directly at Luca. He reached up, grabbed it, and hurled it back to the pitcher in one graceful motion.

"You should be in the game," the Anderson Seminary boy yelled. Luca smiled. Maybe when they saw what he could do, Jake and the guys from Classical would ask him to play.

A girl signaled to Emmy and she left the boys for a few minutes. Luca studied the girl Emmy was talking to. She had long, blond hair, and she looked like a picture of a princess in his favorite book of fairy tales.

When Emmy returned, Luca asked, "Who's the fairy princess you were talking to?"

"That's Missouri Compton. She's a princess all right. At least she thinks so—the princess of Petersburg. That's a good name for her. She's Jake Leighton's girlfriend. They make a good pair."

"What makes you say so?"

"They're both stuck up and stuck on themselves. They're so la-de-dah I could gag."

"Back off. Go away," said Jim, dragging out the words in a way to express his contempt for Emmy's point of view.

Emmy tossed her head. "No, I will not."

Luca thought that Missouri had every right to be stuck up. She was the prettiest girl he had ever seen.

The teams had played for almost an hour and the score was still tied when the sky grew dark, and it began to thunder. A few minutes later, it began to sprinkle. Luca saw a teacher come out of the school with an arm full of student papers.

"Game's over," he said, studying the threatening sky. "You all go home before you get caught in the rain."

The ballplayers groaned. But just then, huge drops of rain began to fall, and everyone ran for cover.

"Run for our porch," Jim yelled and took off for his aunt's house.

Luca turned to Emmy and grabbed her hand. "Come on," he said. "I'll see you home."

The rain fell in sheets, and Jim, Emmy, and Luca were very wet when they reached the porch of the house on Wythe Street.

"Why were we running?" Luca asked, shaking his wet, curly hair.

"We were trying not to get wet," said Emmy with a giggle.

Jim took off his rain-spattered glasses and wiped them on his wet shirt. "Won't you come in?" he asked.

"Can't," said Luca, guessing that Jim was only trying to be polite. "I'm drenched. I'll head home. See you soon." He jumped off the porch right into a big puddle, splashing Jim and Emmy.

Jim jumped into the same puddle. "Got you back," he yelled.

Luca took off at a run. The thunder sounded distant now, but it was still raining heavily. Cool needles of rain stung his face and water dripped from his hair into his eyes. He didn't care. For a few minutes, he had stopped thinking about the appointment with his grandfather.

Chapter 8
Behind the Woodshed

Luca heard the bell on the courthouse strike as he neared his grandfather's big, white house on Saturday morning. He hadn't slept well, dreading the meeting with his grandfather. He slipped through the gate and went around back. The tenth gong was sounding as he came around the corner of the woodshed.

His grandfather was in his shirt sleeves. "Boy, you're on time," he said gruffly. He didn't act surprised.

"Yes, sir." Luca's voice quavered a little and he hoped his grandfather didn't notice and think that he was afraid. "My father taught me to always be on time."

"He should have taught you something about fighting." His grandfather cleared his throat and coughed. "I don't know what gets into boys, but about your age they always seem to get into fights. I guess when your father left for England you hadn't reached that stage yet."

"My mother doesn't believe in fighting, sir."

"Your mother's a strong-minded woman. And I know about strong-minded women. I've married two

39

of them. First your grandmother and then Mrs. S. Mrs. S. had a hissy fit when I went off to the Mexican War."

"You fought in the Mexican War?"

"I surely did. I'll tell you about it sometime. But right now, I need to show you a few things about wrestling. Take off your jacket."

Relief flowed through Luca as he realized that his grandfather wasn't going to punish him. He tore off his jacket and rolled up his shirt sleeves. "Gran...," Luca hesitated, not daring to call the old man grandfather, "what shall I call you, sir?"

The old man thought for a moment. "Gran is fine. Your cousins call me Grandpa, but I can't say I like that much. Makes me sound like an old toadfrog."

"Gran, what if my mother catches me fighting?"

"Boy, I hope you never use the things I'm going to show you. But sometimes you have to stand your ground and fight. We better get at it or Mrs. S. will be out here looking for me. She always manages to find some chore for me to do on Saturday."

Gran grabbed Luca's arm, and before he knew what was happening, Gran had twisted it. Luca's arm was behind his back, and Gran was pressing upward. "I believe this is called a hammerlock." Gran released Luca's arm. "You try it."

Luca hesitated. "Boy," Gran said, "go on, try it. I won't fight back. At least not this time."

Luca took his grandfather's arm and a moment later managed to get it into a hammerlock. "Good," said Gran.

Luca had never seen any boys use a hammerlock, but it was the kind of thing he thought would be good to know. He paid careful attention as Gran walked him through several basic wrestling holds.

"Practice these on one of your friends when you get the chance," Gran said, quite out of breath after his exertion. He leaned against the woodshed, took out his pipe, and lit it.

It was on the tip of Luca's tongue to tell his grandfather that he didn't have any friends, and that Jim Prentice, the only boy who had been friendly, wasn't likely to be a good wrestling partner. Instead, Luca thought he'd use this chance to ask him a question.

"Gran, can I ask you something?"

"Boy, you don't need permission to ask a question. Go ahead. I won't answer it if I don't want to."

"What was my grandmother like?"

Luca's grandfather seemed taken aback. He fiddled with his pipe for a moment. "Well, she looked something like your father. You've probably seen her picture. She was fair. A pretty woman." Gran paused and puffed on his pipe. "I didn't think you favored her until I saw you with those eggs." He chuckled. "You splattered those fellows and then you smiled. It was a crooked, self-satisfied smile. Sometimes she smiled that same way."

"My father never talks about her."

"He was small when she died." Gran knocked the burning tobacco from his pipe. "Next Saturday. Same time."

"Thanks. I'll be here."

"There's one more thing. Not all boys fight clean. And I would be disappointed if I ever heard you were fighting dirty. However, sometimes you have to meet the devil with a pitchfork. You have to do something ungentlemanly to avoid getting beaten to a pulp. So, if that time comes, do whatever it takes. But only as a last resort." Gran put his pipe in his pocket and started to walk toward the house.

Even though they were to meet next week, Luca realized that the chance to talk confidentially with his grandfather might not come again anytime soon. "Gran," he said a bit hesitantly, "would you show me how to shoot? Jake Leighton and Ben McIlwaine have guns of their own, and I've never even held one."

"And why do you want to learn how to shoot?" Gran scowled at Luca. His pleasant manner of a few minutes ago seemed to have vanished.

"I want to be ready if the Yankees come."

"Boy, Yankees don't make war on women and children."

"You told me that sometimes you have to stand your ground and fight," said Luca with more confidence than he felt. He wasn't sure how his grandfather would take being reminded of what he had said. Adults often didn't like it when you remembered their exact words.

"So I did. So I did." Gran shook his head. "I used to hunt all the time with my father when I was your age. I'll think about it."

Chapter 9

Tea at Miss Maizie's

"I'll carry that for you, Madre," said Luca.

"Thank you, Luca," his mother said, handing him the basket containing a dozen fancy, little, Italian-style cakes. Saturday when Luca was out, Eli had come with an invitation for tea on Sunday afternoon, and now they were on their way to visit Miss Maizie.

Luca's mother wore her best blue dress with its wide, hooped skirt, and Luca had carefully slicked down his unruly hair. He wondered if his mother had heard any of the stories about Miss Maizie. He almost said, "We don't need to go to all this bother dressing up for a crazy woman." But he didn't say it because his mother seemed pleased that they had been invited out.

This time, Luca used Miss Maizie's doorknocker. Eli opened the door and led them into Miss Maizie's sitting room. "Hello, hello," said Miss Maizie, rising from her chair. "Mrs. Streetman, it's a pleasure to meet you. So nice of you to come. And Luke. It's good to see you again."

"For you," his mother said, handing Miss Maizie the little cakes she had made.

"How nice, I'll ring for Sara."

Sara appeared instantly, as if she had been waiting just outside. Luca guessed that Sara was a snoop. How else could she know everything that was going on at Miss Maizie's? "We'll have these lovely cakes with our tea at three o'clock," said Miss Maizie.

Luca expected Miss Maizie to start in on Pat once they were comfortably seated. But he was surprised. "What do you know about Garibaldi?" asked Miss Maizie. "I would like to hear all about him." Garibaldi was one of Luca's heroes. One of Italy's heroes. And no one else in Petersburg seemed to know anything about him.

Luca's mother smiled. "I've met him."

"Met him?" Miss Maizie's faded, blue eyes seemed to grow larger. "Oh, tell me about him!"

Madre explained how she had attended a reception for King Victor Emmanuel II with Luca's father, and Garibaldi had been the guest of honor.

"As a general rule, I don't hold with kings," Miss Maizie said. "We have enough problems here just now without kings."

"I'm afraid Giuseppe Garibaldi doesn't like them much either," said Luca's mother. "But he is a true patriot, and he values the unification of Italy more than anything else."

Luca loved the story of Garibaldi and the Thousand Red Shirts. His hero with only a thousand untrained men conquered Sicily and Naples. Then in a supreme gesture, Garibaldi turned his conquests over to the King of Sardinia-Piedmont in the north so that Italy would be unified. Now as Luca listened to his mother telling Miss Maizie all about Garibaldi, he was impressed by how much his mother knew about the great man. He was also surprised by Miss Maizie. She didn't seem crazy at all. In fact, she seemed to already know most of what his mother was telling her.

"How exciting," Miss Maizie said when his mother finished. "I'm afraid seeing my Pat won't be as interesting as meeting Garibaldi."

"I'd love to see Pat," Madre said. Just then, Sara lumbered in with the tea things. As the door closed behind her, Luca caught a glimpse of Eli in the hall.

The conversation turned to a discussion of the shortages of coffee and chocolate, and Luca stopped listening. He imagined he was a famous hero like Garibaldi. Everyone would want to be his friend then. He saw himself astride a great white horse, wearing a Confederate uniform with all the brass buttons shining. He rode up to where Missouri Compton stood, swept off his broad-brimmed hat, and bowed to her.

His daydreaming ended when they finished their tea and cakes, and Miss Maizie took them into the parlor to see Pat. "What an interesting doll!" Madre exclaimed. While she looked at Pat and chatted with Miss Maizie, Luca glanced around. He spotted a straight pin, half-hidden under the rocker of Pat's chair. This made him bolder.

"May I pick her up?" asked Luca. Normally, he wouldn't be caught dead picking up a doll. But he wanted to look at Pat more closely.

Miss Maizie hesitated, and Luca thought he saw her eyes flicker. "Yes, you may," she said. "Pat likes to be picked up."

Luca shot Madre a glance, but she was looking at Miss Maizie. He picked up the doll. Pat was heavier than she looked. He tried to appear casual. He didn't see any pinholes in Pat's face or neck. He turned the doll over in his hand, and he was about to put her back into her little chair when he noticed her dress. There appeared to be lots of tiny holes in it. A chill ran down his spine. What Jordan had told him was true. He put the doll down. Miss Maizie was so busy talking to Madre that he didn't think she had noticed his intense interest.

When they returned to the sitting room, Madre asked, "May I see your garden, Miss Maizie?"

The old woman looked perplexed. Madre explained. "When Eli came with the note, he admired my little garden. I guess you haven't heard that I'm shocking the whole town by working in the vegetables and flowers myself. Eli and I had quite a talk. He's very knowledgeable. I've offered him some of the plants I've grown from seeds my father sent from Italy, and Eli offered me some cuttings and seedlings from your garden."

"Eli is quite a gardener. Of course, you may see it. I dearly love a garden, but I regret to say, I've never done any gardening myself."

Miss Maizie rang for Eli, and he took Luca and Madre to the garden. Miss Maizie watched from the window. "Miss Maizie usually doesn't go outside," Eli said, offering no other explanation.

Later on the walk home, Luca asked his mother, "What did you think of Miss Maizie?"

Madre considered for a moment. "She wasn't what I expected at all. With everyone calling her Crazy Maizie, I feared the worst. She went on a bit too much about Pat, but she seemed sane enough."

"She doesn't go outside. That's pretty strange."

"And I don't think she wanted us to go to the garden. Perhaps she didn't want us to know that she doesn't go outside. I can imagine it would be embarrassing for her to admit such a thing."

"Or maybe she really is crazy," said Luca.

Chapter 10

Payback

"Want to do something?" Jim asked the next day after school.

Luca wasn't eager to be seen all the time with Jim. He still hoped to join Jake Leighton's group. He feared that if he was seen often with Jim, it would ruin his chances. But Jim was waiting for an answer. "Let's practice some of the wrestling holds my grandfather taught me," said Luca, knowing this wasn't the kind of thing that Jim liked to do.

"All right." Jim didn't sound especially enthusiastic. "Let's go to the vacant lot, down the street from my aunt's."

"Lead the way." Luca followed Jim to a weed-filled lot.

Jim took off his jacket and glasses and put them on a pile of brick rubble. "I'm ready," he said. "Show me how."

Luca demonstrated the hammerlock, pinning Jim's arm behind him.

"That hurts," said Jim when Luca released his arm, and before Luca could reply, Jim had grabbed Luca's arm and pinned it behind his back.

"You're a quick learner," Luca said with a laugh when Jim released him.

Luca showed Jim the other holds his grandfather had taught him. They were so intent on their wrestling that they didn't notice the approach of Emmy and Missouri.

"Luca," Emmy called from the sidewalk, "I have someone here who would like to meet you."

Luca and Jim joined the girls. "Missouri," Emmy said, practicing her best manners, "I'd like you to meet Luca Streetman." Missouri held out her hand.

Luca wiped his hands on his pants and extended his hand.

"Luca," Emmy continued without missing a beat, "this is Missouri Compton."

Luca shook Missouri's small, white hand. He looked into her eyes. They were as blue as a bluebird's wing. *"Piacere,"* he blurted out. He instantly realized that he had used Italian instead of English. He felt blood rush to his face. "I mean...nice to meet you," he said, nearly dying with embarrassment.

"The same," replied Missouri. She smiled and her cheeks dimpled.

Luca didn't know what to say next. He was afraid he might say something else stupid. Luckily, Emmy was never at a loss for words. "We're going to see the soldiers. There's a big group passing through town. Want to come?"

Luca looked at Jim, who shrugged his shoulders. "I'll get my stuff," he said. Luca and Jim put on their jackets and picked up their school bags.

"I love seeing our brave soldiers," Missouri purred, addressing no one in particular.

"Where are we going?" asked Jim.

"Courthouse Square," said Emmy, "that's the best place to see what's going on."

Luca tagged along with the others. His cheeks still felt hot, and he was devastated that the prettiest girl he had ever seen probably thought he was a dolt. He listened while Emmy and Missouri talked.

A lot of people were in Courthouse Square watching the soldiers pass through town. Some women threw azalea sprigs to the soldiers. Others offered water and thick ginger cookies. Luca found the crowd comforting. He didn't feel any need to try and talk to Missouri. Line after line of gray-clad soldiers passed the courthouse. Luca noted the odd assortment of uniforms. He had seen soldiers in Italy, and there had been a lot of soldiers in Richmond. But this was the sorriest looking group of fighting men he had ever seen. They were thin, ragged, and dirty. Five musicians had gathered in front of the courthouse. Luca heard a few feeble bars of "Dixie."

"We used to have several good bands in Petersburg," Emmy yelled in his ear, "before the war."

Just then, Missouri saw Jake Leighton farther up the street. She smiled and leaned close to Luca's ear. She said only, "Jake." She gestured and waved to Jim and Emmy and went to join Jake.

Luca, Jim, and Emmy watched the soldiers for a half hour before they grew tired of it. When they were out of the crowd, Emmy parroted Missouri, "I lo-ve seeing our brave soldiers." Then she laughed.

"That isn't very nice," said Luca.

"Go away," said Jim to his sister. He dragged out the words as if he were the lord of the manor and she was a bothersome servant. "Just go away."

Petersburg Courthouse
Courtesy of Petersburg National Battlefield

"I will not go away. Missouri isn't very nice. Her ladyship has condescended to be friendly toward me recently, and that's only because she wanted to meet Luca."

Luca's heart almost stopped when Emmy said again that Missouri had wanted to meet him. The blunder he had made seemed worse than before. When would he stop saying Italian words instead of the proper English?

"Go a-way," said Jim in an annoyed tone of voice. Luca's face flamed when he realized that both Jim and Emmy had seen that he had already fallen under Missouri's spell.

"I won't go away. It's not enough that she has Jake Leighton acting silly over her. She wants Luca to be her slave, too."

"I better go on home," Luca said.

Emmy gave Luca a funny look. "See you tomorrow," Jim said.

"Bye, Emmy, Jim," said Luca, wanting to be alone.

Missouri, Missouri, Missouri, he said the name over and over as he strolled in the direction of High Street. Emmy said Missouri had wanted to meet *him*. If only he hadn't flubbed the introduction, if only he hadn't been suddenly tongue-tied.

Luca had gone several blocks when he heard a whirring sound. A jagged piece of brick flew by his ear. It hit the wall behind him with a clatter. He turned. Freddie Purdy let loose with another brick. Luca ducked.

There was an alley between two buildings on Luca's right. He scooted into it and began to run. Creepy Eddie appeared at the other end of the alley. Luca turned and started back the way he had come. But it was too late. Freddie Purdy was coming after him.

Deciding to take his chances with Eddie at the far end of the alley, Luca ran toward him. Eddie blocked his way. Luca smashed into him, and they both fell down. Luca jumped up. Eddie grabbed Luca's leg, and then Freddie Purdy, coming from the other direction, piled on top of them.

Luca struggled, trying to remember everything Gran had told him. The thought flashed through his head that it might be the time to try something un-gentlemanly. But what? He flailed about trying to fight off the two bullies, but he was outnumbered.

Freddie pinned Luca's arms. "I'll hold him while you tie him up."

Eddie took a length of rope from where it was tied around his waist. Luca struggled, trying to free himself from Freddie's grasp.

"Hold him tighter," Eddie said, as he secured the rope around Luca's wrists.

"I've got a rag to gag him," Freddie said.

Luca instinctively lowered his head and closed his mouth. But that did not prevent Freddie from forcing the filthy rag into his mouth.

"Let's tie him to that post," Freddie said. "Cooling his heels for a while will teach him not to mess with Freddie Purdy."

Luca began struggling again, but Freddie and Eddie dragged him to an upright position and tied his hands to the post. Luca writhed and Freddie laughed.

Eddie left for a moment and came back, holding a jar. "I got these special," he said.

Luca's eyes grew big and he recoiled in horror as Eddie fished a leech out of the jar and placed it on his neck. Luca shuddered, revolted by the thought of the leech sucking his blood. He wanted to scream, but he couldn't with the gag in his mouth. Eddie was taking another leech from the jar when they heard someone coming.

"Let's get out of here," said Freddie. "Come on! This way!" Freddie and Eddie ran toward the far end of the alley. Two men engaged in a heated discussion in the street passed the other end of the alley without glancing into it.

Luca was alone. He twisted his head back and forth, attempting to get rid of the leech and loosen the gag. His hands were tied tightly, and the rope burned his wrists as he tried to wiggle out of it. Tears of anger and frustration sprang to his eyes.

The leech crawled about for a few moments before fixing itself to Luca's neck. He couldn't see the leech, but the thought of the bloodsucking worm made his skin crawl. He wanted to pluck it off and stomp it underfoot. He struggled and struggled, but the ropes held fast. What had he ever done to deserve this?

Chapter 11

Kyle and Jeffie

Luca watched the shadows grow at the end of the alley as the sun sank lower. He tried to calculate how long he had until it would be dark. He wished he had not been so hasty leaving Jim and Emmy. He wished he had been paying attention. If he had been more cautious, he wouldn't have gotten cornered. Why hadn't he taken Freddie's threat more seriously?

Time passed slowly. Luca knew the leech was growing fat on his blood. He tried to think about the blue-green of the Venetian lagoon and the many boats that traversed it night and day, his father in far-off London, and his hero, Garibaldi. Yet he failed to keep his mind off the bloodsucking leech. He squirmed and struggled against the rope that held him.

Suddenly, Luca heard a sound. Voices. Two small black boys came into the alley. They were talking and counting their marbles. They didn't immediately notice Luca who renewed his efforts to dislodge the gag. When one looked up and saw Luca, his eyes grew big. "Look, Jeffie," he said. "Look what somebody did to this boy."

Jeffie looked up. "What are we going to do, Kyle? Should we go get somebody?"

"Naw," said Kyle, "let's just see if we can untie him."

Jeffie reached up and pulled down the rag securing the gag in Luca's mouth. Luca spit out the gag. "Get the leech off me," he tried to say, but his throat was so dry, it came out like a croak. He tried again. This time he yelled, "The leech!"

Just then, Kyle spotted the leech that had grown fat on Luca's blood. "Yuck," said Kyle as he pried it off and threw it on the ground.

"Who did this?" Jeffie asked as he tackled the rope that tied Luca's hands.

"Freddie Purdy," Luca said, recovering his voice a little.

"He's the meanest white boy in town," said Kyle. "Need some help, Jeffie?"

"These knots are pretty tight, but I'm getting them." Jeffie tugged and Luca wriggled his wrists. In a few minutes, he was able to slip his hands out of the rope. He stood for a moment, rubbing his wrists.

"Thank you," Luca said, remembering his manners. He looked for the leech. Spotting it, he stomped on it. His blood spurted out, and he shuddered.

"It was nothing," said Kyle.

"I'm grateful to you both," said Luca, as he walked with the boys to the end of the alley.

"You talk funny," Jeffie said.

"I'm not from here," said Luca.

"Are you from Richmond?" Kyle asked.

"I lived there for a while," said Luca.

"That explains it," said Jeffie.

Back on the street Luca said goodbye to the boys and ran toward High Street. As he neared home, he was relieved to see that his mother was not standing at the gate. When he went inside, Ree was getting ready to leave for the day. It was not yet five o'clock. He hadn't been missed. "Your mother is in the garden with Eli. He brought her some plants. She wants you to write a letter to your father. She's waiting on you to put hers in the mail."

"I'll get right at it," Luca said, "and good night, Ree. See you tomorrow."

Luca bounded upstairs to his room, washed his hands and face, took off his soiled shirt, and put on one with a higher collar. He rubbed his wrists briskly, hoping Madre wouldn't notice the rope burns. He studied the marks the leech had left on his neck in the mirror over his washstand. Fortunately, the shirt collar covered them.

A few minutes later, he was seated at the desk in the parlor in front of a blank sheet of paper. What should he tell his father? What could he tell his father? Madre wrote to his father every day, and each week she sent him a packet of letters, including one from Luca. Madre always read over what Luca wrote, checking his spelling, grammar, and punctuation. And even though he was glad that she caught the errors in his writing, Luca felt that it prevented him from telling his father anything that might upset her.

Luca dipped the pen into the ink, but he couldn't think of what to write. His father had been away a lot the last three years. And yet, it seemed that this time, he was farther away than usual. Since they had moved to Petersburg, life had gotten more complicated, and Luca wished his father would come home for good.

Last week, he had told Father about Miss Maizie and Pat. He sat and thought. He finally decided to tell him about all the soldiers that had passed through town today.

When Luca finished, he added his one page to the many pages his mother had already written and went to look for her. Madre and Eli were bent over a dozen seedlings, planting them in a freshly hoed furrow. Jordan, hoe in hand, stood watching them. They didn't hear Luca approach.

"Miss Maizie says Mr. Streetman's in England," Eli said. Luca noted how carefully and precisely Eli spoke. He sounded more like a minister than a slave.

"Yes," said Madre, "he has an appointment with the Prime Minister on May 15. He still has hopes the British will aid the Confederacy."

Luca wondered if Madre should be telling anyone, even Miss Maizie's trusted slave, what Father was doing in England. And was Eli just making conversation or was there a reason he wanted to know about Luca's father?

"That sounds pretty important," Eli said. It seemed to Luca that Eli was fishing for more information.

"He's part of a delegation representing the Confederacy. I didn't mean to imply that he was going to handle negotiations by himself."

Eli looked up and saw Luca. Eli frowned. "Things are heating up around here," he said.

Luca wondered if Eli had changed the subject after spotting him.

"The war?" Madre asked, not looking up.

"Yes, ma'am, lots of soldiers gathering. Could be a battle shaping up for Petersburg."

"I've heard the rumors," said Madre, planting the last tomato plant. She stood up and saw Luca.

"I'm glad you're home," she said. "Eli has some instructions for you."

Eli tamped dirt around a plant and stood up also. "Master Luca," he said, not looking Luca in the eyes, "Jordan's going to water these each morning for the next couple of weeks, and your mother says you'll take care of them in the evening, just until they take hold. No more than a cup of water on each one. Be careful not to get the leaves wet."

Luca nodded his head, unsure how he should respond to a slave. His mother was so obviously pleased with the garden, he would do all he could to help it grow.

Madre wiped her hands on her apron. "I have some plants for Miss Maizie's garden," she said. "I've put them under the tree. Luca, would you please get that packing box I saved to put them in?"

Luca scurried off and returned moments later with the box. He put the tiny plants into it.

"Remember what I told you about the eggplants," Madre said to Eli. "They like full sun and heat."

"I'm much obliged, ma'am," said Eli, taking the box from Luca.

"I'll have a clump of chives for you next week when I begin clearing out the herb garden," Eli said, as he let himself out their back gate. "In the meantime, take care."

Luca wondered if Madre noticed that there was something menacing in Eli's tone. Was Eli warning or threatening them? Or was it possible that Luca was suspicious of the big man because he was a slave and Luca had little experience dealing with slaves?

Madre took Luca's arm and examined the rope burns. "What happened to your wrist?" she asked.

Luca wanted to tell her everything. About Freddie Purdy, the eggs, Gran, everything. But he was learning that one secret led to another and then another. He didn't want to lie to Madre, but he felt he couldn't tell her the whole truth either. "Some of the guys were just fooling around with a rope." He avoided lying by saying as little as possible.

Madre put his hand down. "Do be more careful," she said.

Luca was glad that Madre didn't ask him anything else. She seemed preoccupied. He wondered if she was worried about the rumors of a Yankee attack on Petersburg.

Chapter 12

Old Men and Young Boys

Gran stood behind the woodshed on Saturday morning, smoking his pipe, waiting for Luca. His jacket hung from the fencepost and his shirt sleeves were rolled up.

"Hello, Gran," said Luca, arriving again just as the clock was striking the hour. He was anxious to tell his grandfather about the encounter with Freddie Purdy.

"Boy," Gran acknowledged Luca's hello with a nod, "how's the wrestling going?"

Luca told him about practicing with Jim and about Freddie and Eddie tying him up.

Gran shook his head. "Have you told anyone about this?"

"I didn't dare tell Madre. She'd be upset if she knew I'd been fighting."

"Don't tell anyone. Everybody flaps their jaws too much in this town. The less said the better. What Purdy wants most of all is for you or your mother or me to make a stink."

"Everybody will find out anyway. Freddie and Eddie will brag."

"But their triumph will lose its sting if you don't react. Act like it was nothing."

"Nothing! It was horrible! I've thought of a thousand ways I could make Freddie and Eddie pay."

"If anyone mentions it to you, smile and shrug. Don't say a word."

"But Gran..."

"Boy, I've lived in this town all my life and I've learned that keeping your trap shut is the surest way to keep stories from circulating."

"I'll do my best," said Luca uncertainly. He wasn't convinced his grandfather was right. But it wouldn't hurt to give it a try.

"So, two little boys untied the knots." Gran paused for a moment while he puffed on his pipe. "Why didn't they use your jackknife?"

"I don't have one."

"I figured as much. A boy without a jackknife is like a wagon without a horse. How can you play mumbly peg without a jackknife?" Gran reached into his pocket and took out a jackknife. "You can have mine."

"I couldn't take your knife," Luca said, shaking his head.

"Boy, I'll get another one."

Luca knew from his grandfather's tone that he had better take the knife. The cool, solid feel of it in his hand gave him courage to ask, "Gran, will you tell me how to play mumbly peg? I've seen Jake Leighton and Ben McIlwaine play. They're good at it. But they'd laugh at me if I asked them about it."

"Boy, give me the knife." Gran shook his head and put his pipe onto the chopping block in front of the woodshed. Luca handed him the knife. Gran opened it. "There are a lot of ways to play mumbly peg and it takes a lot of practice to get good at it. It's been nearly forty years since I've played it, but I suspect I remember the gist of it."

"Why is it called mumbly peg?"

"The boys drive a short stick into the ground with the handle of a jackknife and the loser has to get down and pull it out with his teeth. The peg is usually so far in the ground that the loser has to root around like a pig to pull it out."

"I saw a boy, playing with Jake. His face was all dirty. He must have lost."

"Sure enough. The trick is to get really good at flipping your knife."

Gran put his hand out palm up and placed the knife pointing to the right on his fingers. He decisively flipped the knife and it stuck into the ground.

"Oh," said Luca.

"The first flip is easy. They get harder and harder. Here," Gran said, giving Luca back the knife, "try the first one."

Luca took the knife and tried to imitate his grandfather's easy motion. The knife hit the ground and bounced. "Try again," Gran said. "The knife point has to stick in."

Luca retrieved the knife and flipped it again. This time the knife just barely stuck in the ground.

"Good, " said Gran, "now you're getting the hang of it." He retrieved the knife, transferred it to his left hand and flipped it. Again the knife stuck in the ground. He retrieved the knife and gave it to Luca. "Try the left hand."

Luca tried to imitate Gran's graceful flip. The knife clattered to the ground without sticking in.

"I can see you're going to have to practice," Gran said. "There are as many as twenty-four different positions to flip the knife from. An outstanding player can do all of them. Most players fail to stick the knife in the ground from some of the positions. When that happens, the other players get a turn. Whoever gets through all the positions first, wins. The other gets to root for the peg."

"From watching Jake and others play, I have a general idea of how the game works," said Luca as he picked up the knife and handed it to Gran.

Gran flipped the knife from his right wrist and then his left wrist. Then from his right elbow. He was out of breath and he staggered a little as he bent to pick up the knife. "If I fall over, Mrs. S. will think I've been drinking spirits," he said. "Practice the positions I've shown you. You'll soon get the hang of it." He gave the knife back to Luca.

"Thanks, Gran," said Luca, wondering if he'd ever be able to master the complicated game.

"We'll have no time for a wrestling lesson this morning. They've called up the Petersburg Militia Reserves," Gran said. "Several of us oldsters are meeting at Poplar Lawn Park at 10:30. We're volunteering our services, even though we're over the age limit."

"What's the Petersburg Militia Reserves?"

"Old men and young boys mostly. Boys sixteen and seventeen and men between the ages of forty-five and fifty-five. They call the boys the Junior Reserves. Anyway, the Militia Reserves may be needed to help defend the city." Gran spoke cheerfully, but Luca noticed his grandfather seemed distressed.

"Can I go too?"

"Thank God, they're not taking boys your age. But I have decided it's time you learned to shoot. When I was a boy, a youngster your age could put meat on the table."

"When do we start?" asked Luca enthusiastically.

"Hold on there a moment, boy. We'll have to go someplace outside of town. I'll make the arrangements. Let's see, can you meet here at four on Tuesday?"

"Of course," said Luca, trying not to sound too excited.

Gran smiled and gave Luca a pat on the shoulder. "Run along now. I've got to meet the others."

It was only 10:20, and Luca had the rest of the morning free. He decided to go and see Jim. Maybe he would want to do something. Luca went to Jim's aunt's house. A barrel-shaped woman sat in a rocker on the front porch talking to a pale, thin woman, wrapped in a blanket.

Luca approached the porch. "Excuse me, ma'am," he said, addressing the heavy-set woman. The woman stopped talking and looked in his direction.

"May I help you?" she said.

"I'm Luca Streetman, one of Jim's friends. Is Jim here?"

"Oh, yes, the Streetman boy. Jim and Emmy have told me about you. Jim isn't here," said the other woman. "I'm Jim's mother."

"How do you do, ma'am," said Luca.

"Jim's at Poplar Lawn watching the Militia Reserves muster," said his aunt.

"Thank you, ma'am," Luca said, "I'll go look for him." He headed in the direction of the city park.

A few minutes later, he came to Poplar Lawn where a group of men and older boys were gathered on the grass. In addition to the hundred or so men and boys, there were at least as many spectators loitering on the edge of the park.

The militia was just standing around. A knot of professional men stood together. Luca recognized Cadaver Barnum, old thin-lips, and Mr. Dupuy, the principal from his school. He saw Mr. McIlwaine, Ben McIlwaine's father, who owned McIlwaine's General Store and a man he knew to be Jim's Uncle Pete. His grandfather was talking with several men whom Luca guessed must be bankers because they all wore similar business suits. Half a dozen older boys from Classical were milling about. Jake and Ben stood near them, even though they weren't officially old enough to belong to the militia. A few men on the field carried guns, but it looked more like a gathering for a Sunday school picnic than a military muster. Nothing much seemed to be going on.

Finally, an officer with a full, black beard and a gray uniform called out, "AttenSHUN!" The men on the field stopped talking and formed two ragged lines, facing the officer. "That's all for today. Next Saturday we'll drill with weapons. We'll issue firearms to anyone who doesn't have one. Militia Reserves disMISSED!"

As the crowd began to disperse, Luca saw Emmy with a group of girls. One of them was Missouri Compton. Jake Leighton stood just in front of Luca, talking to Ben. They didn't see him. Luca was just about to join them when he heard his name mentioned.

"I thought for a while Streetman might be one of us," said Jake.

"So did I," said Ben. "But now that he's hanging around with that loser Jim Prentice, I'm ready to write him off...permanently."

"They make a good pair, a brain and a foreigner," said Jake. He laughed. "I wonder what they find to talk about."

Luca's face flamed. He slipped away, feeling awful. He was tired of always being an outsider. He didn't want to talk to anyone. Not even Jim. Especially not Jim. The group might have accepted him, if he hadn't become friends with Jim.

Chapter 13

At the Foundry

"You'll never guess what happened last night," Jim said several days later as he and Luca were walking home from school..

"Mrs. Connolly's cow got away again?" replied Luca, remembering an incident from his first week in Petersburg when town boys had chased a runaway cow through the streets.

"No, Henry Clay Pate is back in town."

"So?"

"I forgot, you wouldn't know about Pate. He's a lawyer and an engineer. He was a friend of my father's. He came to visit my mother last night."

"So?" Luca wondered why this was so important.

"So, Pate must be working on another secret weapon."

"Secret weapon?" asked Luca with more interest.

"Pate invented a revolving cannon. Two of them were made right here in Petersburg. The first one exploded. Killed three men. The other one's still here."

"And you think he might have a new invention?"

Henry Pate's Revolving Cannon
Courtesy of the Petersburg Museums, City of Petersburg

"He told my mother he was in town on business. Let's go to the foundry. See what's going on."

The boys walked in the direction of Tappey's foundry. Luca spotted Freddie Purdy across from Jarratt's Hotel. Freddie turned up another street. The story of Luca's misadventure with Freddie and Eddie had been the source of a great deal of gossip for several days. Jake and several other boys had asked Luca about it, but he had shrugged it off with a smile. Like his grandfather had predicted, interest in the affair soon died. Luca wasn't sure why, but ever since then, Freddie had steered clear of him. Perhaps he couldn't understand why Luca had taken the matter so lightly. Whatever the reason, Luca was glad that Freddie was avoiding him.

Luca and Jim neared Market Street. The streets were crowded with soldiers and workmen. A wagon, heavily laden with barrels, rumbled by. Another wagon was being loaded by a crane that creaked as it lowered bulky boxes into the wagon bed. No one paid any attention to Luca and Jim. When they reached the foundry, they paused. "What do we do now?" asked Luca.

The wide doors of the foundry were open to the street, and several blacksmiths, wearing leather aprons, could be seen working at the forges. Nothing unusual seemed to be going on.

"Let's hang around a little. We don't have anything to do anyway. Maybe we'll see Pate."

"I've got a ball." Luca reached into his book bag. "Here, catch."

They tossed the ball back and forth in front of the foundry. When they tired of playing catch, they sat on the gray-stone steps of the tobacco warehouse across the street. Between the hammering of the blacksmiths and the clanging of the heavy machinery in the foundry, it was difficult to talk.

"I guess this wasn't a good idea," said Jim after a while. "Nothing seems to be going on."

Luca was about to agree when he saw Eli coming up the street. "Let's stay a few more minutes. How about some wall ball?" Luca got up and started tossing the ball against the wall of the warehouse. Jim joined him.

As they played, Luca was careful to seem like he was intently interested in the game. He kept an eye on Eli, wondering what he was doing in this part of town. Was it a coincidence that he just happened to visit the foundry on a day when the weapon specialist Henry Pate was in town?

Jim slammed the ball hard, and Luca failed to catch it. "Good lick," he said.

"I'm getting better," said Jim, looking pleased that he had outplayed Luca.

Eli went into the foundry and didn't come out. "One more game," said Luca. "I need a chance to even the score."

Jim could hardly refuse since he had just won. He threw the ball at the wall. Luca caught it easily, and Jim ran to retrieve Luca's next throw. Jim hurled the ball at the wall.

Luca lunged and failed to catch it. The ball skittered across the street and into the foundry through the open doors. Luca ran after it, slowing as he neared. The ball had come to rest about two yards inside. He looked around. One of the blacksmiths was talking with Eli. The others were working. No one seemed to notice Luca except Eli. He was scowling, whether at Luca or what the blacksmith was saying, Luca wasn't sure. He retrieved the ball and stepped out into the late afternoon sunshine.

What was Eli up to? Had he heard about Henry Pate's return to Petersburg and made up a reason to go to the foundry? Was he trying to see if Pate had a new invention? Luca was tempted to share his suspicions with Jim on the way home. But he felt a little foolish. Freddie Purdy had called him a Yankee spy, and Luca thought he probably had spies on his mind. It didn't mean that the town was full of Yankees and spies, or did it?

Chapter 14

Sunday Dinner

"Must I wear my jacket?" Luca asked the following Sunday.

"I don't want your father's family to think that we don't know how to dress for Sunday dinner," said Madre.

"But it's so hot," Luca lamented, putting on his woolen dress-up jacket.

"This hot spell will be good for the garden. Come along now or we'll be late."

Luca felt apprehensive as they walked to his grandfather's house. He hadn't told Madre about the knife or his grandfather's agreeing to teach him to shoot. He knew she wouldn't approve. He was pretty sure Gran wouldn't say anything about the upcoming target practice. But since all the other boys had knives, perhaps Gran wouldn't realize that Madre felt about knives the way she felt about fighting.

The large, dark parlor with its red-velvet curtains and heavy oak furniture was already filled with people when Luca and his mother arrived. His Aunt Cornelia and her girls, four and six years old, wearing frilly

Sunday dresses, sat on the horsehair sofa. The girls' three-year-old brother was sitting on the floor near the sofa, playing with blocks. The children's father, Luca's uncle, was an adjutant to General Lee, and he was off fighting with the Army of Northern Virginia. Luca's Aunt Lucy sat on the piano stool. Her five-year-old twin girls were drawing at a small table. Their father was in the Petersburg Grays, and he also was away with the army. Luca's step-grandmother, Mrs. S., as Gran called her, was a petite woman with gray hair captured in a decorative net at the nape of her neck. She flitted from person to person. Something about Mrs. S. reminded Luca of a little bird. Perhaps it was her bright eyes and cheerful manner.

"I'm so glad you could come," Mrs. S. said, speaking in the soft, rich tones of a Southern lady.

Luca and his mother sat on a small, green velvet sofa. "There's something we've been wanting to discuss with you, Angelica," Aunt Lucy said to Luca's mother after they had exchanged the usual pleasantries about the sultry weather.

"What's that?" asked Luca's mother, raising one eyebrow.

"We know that you speak Italian. We're wondering if you speak French, too?"

"Why, of course. I went to finishing school in France."

"We know how you feel about the war," Aunt Lucy said with some hesitation. Her pretty face clouded with concern. "But there are some French-speaking Confederate soldiers from Louisiana in the hospital, and the doctors need someone who can communicate with them. Perhaps even write letters home for them."

"I'd be glad to help. In fact, I've wanted to volunteer at one of the hospitals. But since no one had asked me, I was afraid my help wouldn't be welcome."

Aunt Lucy's face relaxed in a smile. "There are nearly three thousand men now in the city hospitals, and we urgently need help. We haven't asked you before because we wanted you to have a chance to settle in before we recruited you."

"When do I begin?"

"As soon as you're able to spare the time. I could take you there tomorrow and introduce you to everyone."

"That'll be fine. Perhaps you can fill me in on what the local women are doing to help the wounded men."

Luca's aunts began telling his mother about the various groups of women in town and what they were doing. Luca feared he was in for a long, boring afternoon. He regretted that none of his cousins were his age. He wished he was young enough to get down on the floor with his cousin Joey and play blocks. Instead, he just sat on the uncomfortable sofa and listened to the women. He was only half paying attention. His aunts had ended the discussion about the hospitals and now were gossiping. When he heard his Aunt Cornelia mention the Trapezium House, he became alert. He had heard about the house from the boys at school.

"Mrs. Stokes saw a light there," said Aunt Cornelia. "She swears to it. She wasn't imagining it."

"You don't say," said Mrs. S. Her eyes grew big. "That place is evil. I know it. I've always known it."

"Now, Mother," said Aunt Lucy, "you know that Boadicea with all her herbs and voodoo lived there for years. That's why the place has such a bad name."

"It's more than that," Mrs. S. said firmly. She suddenly realized that Luca's mother might not know what they were talking about. "You know that odd house downtown. The one that is called the Trapezium House. It was owned by a man named O'Hara."

"Yes, I know the one you mean," said Luca's mother. "I've often wondered about it."

"It has no perpendicular lines in it. The story is that O'Hara's servant—she's a free woman who sells herbs and potions—came from the West Indies. She convinced him that squared corners housed evil spirits," said Aunt Lucy.

"Everything in the house is off balance," said Aunt Cornelia. "And the people who have lived there have been off balance too."

"Have you ever been inside?" asked Madre.

Aunt Cornelia visibly recoiled at the thought. "No, and I don't intend to ever cross the threshold. I agree with Mother. It's an evil place, filled with darkness and despair," she said.

"It looks like the house has been there for a while," said Madre. "The herb woman must be pretty old."

"Boadicea must be eighty years old or older," Mrs. S. said. "She lives by herself in a shack out in the woods. Her daughter's here in town. She's a free woman, too. Her name's Sara. She works for Miss Maizie."

The topic of conversation shifted.

"I wish Mr. S. wasn't involved with the Militia Reserves. He's well over age fifty-five. No one expects him to fight," Mrs. S. said.

"Now, Mother," Aunt Cornelia said, "he does have more military experience than most of the townspeople."

"I've tried to talk some sense into him. But he just gets ornery and refuses to talk about it," Mrs. S. said, shaking her head in exasperation.

Then the women began to discuss the shortages of lace and French fabrics caused by the Union blockade of Confederate ports. Luca stopped listening and thought over what he had heard about the peculiar Trapezium House. He had studied trapezoids in school, and he had stood outside the Trapezium House, trying to guess its floor plan. He had been interested to hear the house was connected—however distantly—to Sara who worked for Miss Maizie. And Sara was related to a woman who was supposed to be a witch. Now he knew why Sara made him uneasy. He was mulling that over when Gran came into the parlor and greeted everyone. He didn't sit down. He just stood by his wife's chair.

"Sunday dinner's like a hen party these days," he said.

Mrs. S. laughed her little laugh. "It's a good thing you like women."

"That I do," said Gran with a bow to the ladies. "But I have to see a man about a horse. Will you excuse me? I'll be back for dinner." He headed for the front door. Then he stopped and turned to Luca. "Boy, you better come along. There's no telling what you'll hear with all these ladies gossiping to beat the band."

Luca leapt to his feet. Then, remembering his manners, he looked in Madre's direction. She nodded her head. He turned to the others. "If you'll excuse me, I'll be back for dinner," he said. Before he reached the door, the women had resumed their conversation.

"Thanks, Gran," said Luca when they were well away from the house.

"Think nothing of it," said his grandfather, twisting his mustache absent-mindedly as they walked along. "I'd rather kiss a polecat with his hackles up than be stuck in the house all Sunday afternoon."

"Where are you going to see this man about a horse?"

Gran laughed. "There are darn few horses left in town. Actually, the phrase 'see a man about a horse,' is a polite way of making an exit. That's all."

There was much Luca didn't understand about customs in Petersburg, and the Trapezium House was still on his mind. "What's voodoo, Gran?"

"It's a kind of religion," said Gran without hesitation. "A lot of people believe in it."

"Did Mr. O'Hara, who built the Trapezium House, believe in it?"

"It's hard to say. Some people claim that he built the Trapezium House in that shape because that was the shape of the lot."

"What do you think?"

"I knew O'Hara. He dealt with Farmers Bank. He seemed a reasonable-enough fellow. But you never know what goes on in people's heads."

"What else do you know about voodoo?" asked Luca, still unsatisfied.

"I've heard there are charms and spells connected to it. Those people who practice voodoo use animal parts and herbs to concoct potions of various sorts."

"It sounds like witchcraft. I thought that went out of style about two hundred years ago."

"Don't be too quick to write off herbs and potions," said Gran. "We live in an age of science and learning, but many people still can't read and write.

Their world is frightening and often miserable, not to mention unfair. Many people are too poor to afford modern doctoring, so they seek the remedies that are available. And sometimes those remedies work. At least they work enough to keep Boadicea and her ilk in business."

"Is voodoo only selling herbs and potions?"

"There's more to it than that. I'm not sure what else they do, but I have heard that they make dolls and stick pins in them. And the pins cause pain or even death."

"Do they, really?"

"I believe people *think* they cause harm."

Luca wanted to ask Gran more about voodoo in Petersburg, but they had arrived at Courthouse Square and walked one block beyond to Corling's Corner. Other men, also refugees from the Sunday afternoon visiting that preceded Sunday dinner, had gathered there to discuss the war. The townsmen were listening to a grizzled soldier in a shabby, gray uniform.

"There are Union troops arriving at City Point, and if more come, we're in trouble," the soldier said.

An officer with his arm in a sling spoke up, "We don't have enough men to defend Petersburg. Even though we're the second largest city in Virginia, most of our men are away fighting with the Confederacy. There's only the 46th Virginia, one company of the 23rd South Carolina, one cavalry regiment, one artillery battery, and two groups of militia."

"And the Petersburg Militia Reserves," said Gran.

The men roared with laughter. "The Milita Reserves are a joke," one scoffed.

"I hope they remain a joke. I hate to think that we might actually go into battle," said Gran.

"It's rumored that General Wise has sent a message to General Lee, pleading for more men," said the officer. "With any luck, we won't need civilians."

Several men started to talk at once and the gathering broke into small groups, all of them discussing the war. While Gran was busy talking to the officer, Luca looked around. Most of the townsmen were older men, gray-haired and pot-bellied. There were a few Confederate soldiers, professional men, and older boys.

A man wearing an elegant, beige suit caught Luca's eye. His face was flushed and his eyes were red. Noting his limp, Luca guessed it was Jordan's employer, Carter Wiley. He had quite a reputation around town as a drinker and a ne'er-do-well.

A group of African American men stood nearby. One looked familiar. He was a big man whose back was to Luca. When the man turned around, Luca saw it was Eli.

Chapter 15

Jim's Gun

"We didn't even fire the gun," Luca said to Jim on Wednesday afternoon. "My grandfather showed me how to take the gun apart and clean it. We spent forty-five minutes cleaning the darn gun."

"Good, you can help me clean my father's gun. It's stored in the stables behind my aunt's house along with our household goods. It must be in bad shape. I don't think anyone has even looked at it since we moved here three years ago."

"All right," said Luca, curious to see the gun. "How did you learn to shoot?"

"My father taught me. Before the war we lived in the Shenandoah Valley. Most of the boys there learn to shoot as soon as they're big enough to hold a gun. But that was some time ago." Jim stared off into space and was quiet.

They walked in silence until they reached the stables behind Jim's house. The light was dim inside, and the building smelled of rotting hay and horse manure. "No one comes here much now," said Jim. "The army has confiscated the horses."

"Did they pay for them?"

"Sort of," said Jim, "in Confederate dollars. The Confederacy has printed so much money that people have to pay ten dollars for what would have cost one dollar before the war. They have even printed dollars here in Petersburg." Jim reached into his pocket and showed one to Luca. "I don't know if you've ever noticed, but the Exchange Building is on the Petersburg dollar." Luca took the Petersburg dollar and examined it.

"I wondered why things are so expensive." Luca handed Jim back the dollar.

"The gun's over here." Jim turned to packing boxes stacked off to one side. He pried off the top of one box and took out a gun wrapped in a cloth.

"What kind of gun is it?" asked Luca, as he watched Jim unwrap the funny-looking weapon.

"This dates from the War of 1812. It's a flintlock rifle. It originally belonged to my great uncle. He was at the Battle of New Orleans, where Andrew Jackson defeated the British." Jim handed Luca the gun.

Luca turned the rifle over in his hands. "It's a fine rifle," he said, thinking that it looked a little rusty.

"I've got oil and rags. Let's see what we can do to clean it."

Luca sat next to Jim in the musty-smelling hay and watched as Jim tried to take the gun apart. "I should have cleaned this before," said Jim as he struggled with the gun.

"I wanted to tell you about...," Luca paused. What did he want to tell Jim about his visits to Miss Maizie? Were his suspicions of Eli ridiculous?

"What?" asked Jim, looking up from his task.

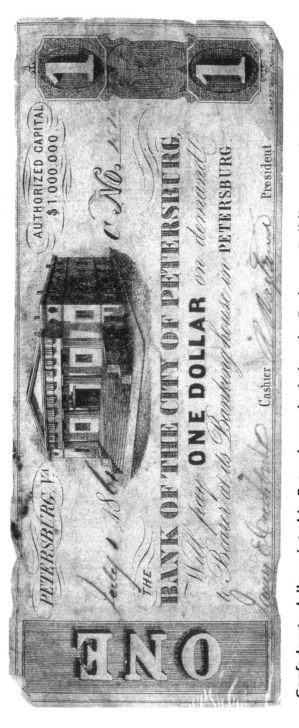

Confederate dollar minted in Petersburg, depicting the Exchange Building, now the Siege Museum

Courtesy of the Petersburg Museums, City of Petersburg

Luca had mentioned visiting Miss Maizie, but he hadn't told Jim everything. Now he told Jim about the pins, Sara's relationship to Mr. O'Hara's slave, his suspicion that Eli might be a spy, the Trapezium House, and what he knew about voodoo. "Am I imagining all this," he concluded, "or is something strange going on?"

Jim stopped his work on the gun. "It sounds awfully suspicious to me. Something strange is going on. I don't think you're imagining it."

"What do you make of it?"

"I don't know. But maybe you and I can find out. Strange things have been going on for so long at Miss Maizie's that folks have stopped paying attention."

"Jim, I'm new here, so I don't have any background. Let's begin by you telling me everything you know about Miss Maizie."

"Well, like everyone else, I haven't thought much about Miss Maizie. Let me see..." Jim thought for a moment before continuing. "My Uncle Pete is Miss Maizie's lawyer. And not long ago, he went to her house. Something about changing her will. Her husband left her a wealthy woman when he died."

"Does she have any children?"

"She had a baby, but it died within weeks of when it was born. It was a girl, I think."

"Well, who'll inherit her property?"

"She has a distant relative, Carter Wiley, the grandson of her cousin Jane."

"So why would she change her will?"

"I don't know. Of course, Uncle Pete doesn't talk about stuff like this. But I know that people change their wills a lot. They sell or buy something, more land, whatever, and then they have to update the wills. In fact, with the fear that the bluecoats will attack Petersburg soon, Uncle Peter has been busy lately with wills."

"How good is a will made by a crazy person?"

"I don't know, but I guess we'll find out someday."

"What do you know about Eli?"

"Not much, except I've always known he's one smart fellow. He handles all of Miss Maizie's business, for one thing. It's no secret that Miss Maizie trusts Eli completely."

"I hope her trust is not misplaced," said Luca, thinking about the fragile, dotty, old woman.

"That's all I know about Miss Maizie." Jim looked down at the gun and put down the oily rag.

"This gun needs a lot more work," Luca said as he examined the pitted metal of the barrel.

"We'll have to spend more time on it sometime soon. Right now, I'm more interested in getting to the bottom of whatever is going on at Miss Maizie's." Jim placed the gun carefully back into the packing box.

"Me too, and it's time I headed on home." Luca got up and brushed hay from his pants.

Luca was almost at the door when Jim said, "There's one more thing. I've heard Sara has some hold on Miss Maizie. I don't know what it is, but I don't like that woman."

"I know what you mean. When she's around, it's like there's a dark cloud over everything."

Chapter 16

Fishing

"I know how to load a gun now," Luca said several days later as he and Jim left school. "I wonder if Gran's ever going to let me actually shoot it."

"You have to know the stuff your grandfather is teaching you," Jim said.

"What good is it all if I don't know how to shoot the blasted thing!"

"I'm sure you'll get to fire it soon." Jim opened a book that he was holding and began leafing through it, deep in thought.

Luca waved his hand in front of Jim's face. Jim looked up and grinned. "Do you want to do something this afternoon?" Luca asked.

Jim closed the book and stuck it in his book bag. "I promised Emmy we'd do something. Before you and I became friends, Emmy and I did a lot more things together. Do you want to join us?"

"I don't think Emmy likes me."

"I'm sure she does."

"Well, she sure doesn't act like it."

"That's how I know she likes you. She only picks on people she likes. Let's go to my house and see what she has in mind."

On the way to his house, Jim asked, "What will you do when school's out?"

"My mother has plans for me." Luca made a face. "She wants me to work on my Italian. She's afraid I'm losing my ability to read and write it. What'll you do?" Luca looked expectantly at Jim.

"I'm going to help Uncle Pete mornings in his law office. He's short-handed because of the war. First one, then another of his clerks joined the army. So, I'm going to file papers and copy letters. Run errands. That sort of thing."

"And Emmy?"

"Emmy will be over at our Aunt Rachel's house helping to mind my cousins so my Aunt Rachel can go to Tabb Street Church with my Aunt Mary Louise to make bandages."

"Did I hear my name mentioned?" Emmy asked, joining them.

"I was just telling Luca how you'll be at Aunt Rachel's when school's out," said Jim.

"You boys are lucky," Emmy said. "You don't get stuck with minding babies."

"I thought girls liked messing around with babies. You know, girl stuff," said Luca. He looked at her with a serious expression. He was learning how to deal with Emmy.

"Go away," Emmy said, exaggerating the words and sticking out her tongue at him. "Just go away. Changing babies and wiping noses is boring, boring, boring."

Luca laughed. "What would you like to do?"

"Anything but mind Aunt Rachel's spoiled brats," Emmy said as they reached the house.

"What would you like to do today?" Jim asked.

"Let's go down to the river," Emmy said. "Throw in a couple of lines and see if we catch anything."

"I know where some bamboo is growing," said Jim. "Maybe we can cut some poles."

"There's a hatchet in the kitchen. The cook uses it to chop kindling for the cookstove. I'll get it while you get the gear from the barn," Emmy said.

"This time of year there is usually somebody down by the river selling worms. All we'll need is a few pennies' worth," said Jim.

Emmy turned to Luca. "Do you want to come along?"

"I've never gone fishing," said Luca. "Since ladies aren't supposed to garden, I'm surprised that girls are allowed to fish."

"Miss Missouri Compton wouldn't be caught dead with a fishing pole. That's for sure. She's too much the princess," said Emmy.

"Go away, Emmy," said Jim, drawing out the words in his most patronizing tone of voice.

"Okay, fishing is fine with me, but you'll have to show me how," said Luca, somewhat put off by Emmy's remarks about Missouri. Emmy was purposely antagonizing him because she suspected he was sweet on Missouri. Going to an all-boys school, Luca wasn't used to being around girls, especially girls with minds of their own like Emmy.

Half an hour later, they found a spot along the bank of the Appomattox River. Spring runoff made the river more turbulent than usual, and the water splashed

Johnson's Mill on the Appomattox River
Courtesy of Petersburg National Battlefield

and gurgled across rocks and broken branches as it made its way downriver. "This was once part of a mill," said Jim, settling himself on an old brick wall near the water's edge.

Jim gave Luca the lesson on how to bait the hook. "Disgusting," Luca said, as he skewered the worm.

"The difficult part of the whole thing is what you do now," Emmy said.

"What's that?" asked Luca, pushing his dark hair from his forehead.

"Wait."

"I imagine it's especially difficult for you," said Luca. He smiled his crooked smile.

Emmy made a face. "Go away," she said, adopting the exasperated tone of voice that Jim always used when he wanted her to stop whatever she was doing.

The three of them sat on the wall watching their lines. Jim was the first to get a nibble, but when he pulled the line from the water, there was nothing on it.

A moment later, Emmy yanked up her line. There was a tiny sunfish on the end of the hook. "He's a monster," she said.

Jim grabbed the line, removed the little fish, and threw it back. Emmy baited her hook again and put the line in the river.

They sat talking quietly and listening to the splash of the water as it hit the bricks they were sitting on. Finally, Jim stood up. "I've had enough. The fish aren't biting. At least not here."

"Let's see if anybody else along the river has caught anything," said Emmy, getting up and pulling her line out of the water.

They walked along the river until they came to two old men fishing. "Have you caught anything?" Jim asked as they approached.

"Sure have," said the taller of the two men. He pulled up a line on which there was a large catfish.

The catfish flapped about and seemed to be staring at them with its glassy eyes. "It sure is big and ugly," said Luca.

"I've promised it to Miss Maizie's Sara," said the tall man. "She's been wanting a fish without scales. And I've got her a good one."

Luca gave Jim a quizzical look. They were almost back to the street that ran along the river when Jim said, "I wonder what Sara wants with that fish. Not everybody likes it. I wonder if it is something Miss Maizie eats."

Chapter 17

May 5

Mr. Dupuy, the principal, came to the door of Luca's classroom the morning of May 5, and Mr. Barnum stepped out and disappeared down the hall. The students began to talk.

"I wonder what's going on," Luca said. "It has to be important for old Cadaver to leave without saying a word."

"I don't know what's going on," said Jim. "But lately everybody's talking about an attack on the city."

The courthouse bell began to clang. The boys leapt to the windows to look out. Everyone began talking at once. Luca saw people rushing toward Courthouse Square.

Mr. Barnum came back into the classroom. He banged his ruler on the desk. "Quiet," he said in his usual funereal voice, and for once, he was obeyed immediately. "Forty thousand Federals have landed at City Point, seven miles away. They may be headed for the city. Our Confederate general in charge, General Pickett, is calling out the Militia Reserves." Barnum paused for a second. "The situation is grave. General

Pickett is preparing to defend the city and is asking that anyone fourteen or older join the Militia Reserves."

"Hurrah!" someone shouted.

"Anyone eligible should go to the courthouse immediately. Class dismissed," said Mr. Barnum, hurrying from the room.

Most of the boys in Luca's class were fourteen. "Are you coming?" Jim shouted to Luca as they rushed outside with the others. "I'm going home for my gun."

Luca shook his head. He hadn't told Jim that he was two years younger than everyone else, and before he could say anything, they were separated.

The students streamed toward the center of town, carried on a great wave of excitement. Luca went along with them, but hung back, watching people converge on the courthouse from every direction.

It seemed that the whole town had turned out, even Carter Wiley, unshaven and still in his evening clothes. Courthouse Square was full of people, all milling around. As Luca watched, soldiers in gray uniforms began corralling the men and boys. His grandfather was helping Major Archer by giving out guns to those who didn't have them. Luca noted the odd assortment of firearms, some of unfamiliar shapes and sizes.

The situation was urgent. Things happened quickly. It was less than an hour later when Luca followed the Militia Reserves out of town. So much was going on that no one paid him any attention. As they headed for the Dimmock Line, a lone drummer beat a cadence. The deep growl of the drum lent an air of seriousness to the undertaking.

Typical Virginia earthworks
Drawing by W. L. Sheppard in *The Century*, 30 (June, 1885), p. 297

The Militia Reserves halted near the Jordan farm at Battery 5 on the Dimmock Line, two miles from town. Luca had been impressed with the Dimmock Line when Jim had first taken him to see it. Now the earthworks didn't look high enough to offer much protection from an attack and the gun emplacements on the battery appeared to be empty. He watched as the men and boys took their positions behind the earthworks and prepared to defend the road that led from City Point to Petersburg.

It was a curious sight. Few men were in uniform. No battle flags fluttered in the morning breeze. There were none of the trappings that made war heroic in parades and in colored picture books. Most of the men wore whatever they had worn to work that morning. Lawyers and bankers in suit coats stood beside factory and textile mill workers in aprons and shirt sleeves.

Luca recognized Mr. McIlwaine from the General Store, standing beside his butcher, who still wore an apron.

Luca stayed behind a massive oak tree near the Jordan farm, well out of sight. He spotted Jim and other boys from Classical behind the earthworks, and he wished he was with them. A knot grew in his stomach. What would Jake and the others think of him now? They'd surely think he was a coward. Or worse. They'd think he really was a traitor, a Yankee sympathizer, or even a spy. For the first time he wondered what Jim would think of him. The boy who so often looked foolish now seemed as serious and as solid as stone.

As one of the few older men with military experience, Luca's grandfather was in the thick of the activity. He traversed the area with the officers, his head bent as he listened to Major Archer giving commands to the militiamen.

It wasn't long before everyone and everything was in place. But nothing happened. Luca waited and watched. An hour passed, and then two. Because he was by himself, Luca had no idea what was going on. He worried that if he went home, he would miss the attack.

As the morning wore into afternoon, Luca noticed that everyone manning the breastworks stayed in their positions, but let down their guard. When it was mid-afternoon and there was still no sign of a Yankee attack on Petersburg, he decided to go home. Since his mother had started helping at the hospital, Luca took a lunch to school and no longer went home at noon. But he knew his mother would be getting home from the hospital soon, and he wanted to be there when she arrived. She would be worried if she didn't find him at home. He'd return to Battery 5 later.

Luca's mouth was dry and his stomach grumbled as he made his way back to town. The road was dry, and he breathed in the dust as he walked. He met a few people headed toward the Dimmock Line. They were probably as curious as he had been about what was going on.

Suddenly, out of the corner of his eye, Luca spotted Eli. Luca was immediately alert, as if some animal instinct swung into operation. Eli carried a basket and had left the main road to follow a narrow path through the brambles. Where was he going? With all of Petersburg in arms, what errand could be important enough to take Eli away from Miss Maizie's house?

Luca decided to follow him. He wasn't sure why, but something told him it was the thing to do.

Eli had disappeared into the thick undergrowth. Luca left the main road. He was not a sneak by nature, but curiosity and suspicion took hold of him. Eli was up to something. Luca intended to find out where Eli was going and why.

Luca didn't have to go far. The brush opened into a clearing about a half mile from the road. In the clearing was an unpainted cabin and a lean-to. The lean-to was about fifty yards from the shack and held rotting cordwood. Luca scooted behind a derelict farm wagon. Its warped wood had faded to gray and was barely visible amid the brambles that covered it. It was an ideal place to watch Eli without being seen.

Eli took several onions out of his basket and placed them in a pile at his feet. Then he took out a leather pouch. He went to the lean-to and stuffed the pouch between two logs. He put the onions back into the basket and a moment later was on the path back to the road.

Luca didn't know what to do. Should he get the pouch and see what was in it? He was hesitant to take something that didn't belong to him. Yet, what if Eli was a spy? Perhaps the pouch contained a message for the Yankees. Or was it just some voodoo favor he was doing for Sara? It seemed like an odd day to be doing anything that wasn't absolutely necessary.

Luca waited for a few minutes to see if anyone came to claim the pouch. No one entered the clearing. The shadows were deepening, and Luca knew he should go home before he had to explain why he was late. He followed the path back to the road, still unsure what to do about Eli.

"Where's Madre?" Luca asked Ree when he arrived home. She was sitting in the kitchen shelling peas at the kitchen table.

"She came home a while back. Told me I could go along home soon as you got here," said Ree. "She's staying at the hospital. There's a big battle going on somewhere east of here and they're expecting a train-load of wounded sometime soon."

Ree put away the peas, took off her apron, and got ready to leave for the day. "Thanks for waiting," said Luca. "There's so much excitement going on, I guess I'm a little late."

"Your mama left bread and cold chicken for you. I'll fix it, if you want."

"That's all right. I'll manage." It was obvious that Ree was eager to leave. "I'll see you tomorrow."

The door banged as Ree left. Luca went to the water bucket that stood beside the table in the kitchen. He drank two dippers full without bothering to get a cup or glass. Then he cut a slab of his mother's good bread, found the sliced chicken, and placed it across the yeasty-smelling bread.

Half an hour later, Luca left again. He wanted to see what was happening at Battery 5. It was late afternoon and the town seemed quiet after the excitement earlier in the day. As Luca neared the outskirts of town, he strained to see if he could hear the sound of battle. But he heard no cannon or rifle fire.

People were coming from the general direction of Battery 5. As Luca drew nearer, he saw a group of boys headed back to town. One of the boys was Jake Leighton.

"Hey, Jake," Luca called, "what's happening?"

"They're sending back some of the Militia Reserves," Jake said. He spoke slowly as if he was extremely tired. "Boys mostly. The others will spend the night. Everyone's saying that it was a false alarm. No bluebellies anywhere about. How come you're going the wrong way?"

Luca took a deep breath. He was on the spot and didn't know what to say. "My mother, she's against... *combattimento*." He had meant to say fighting, but he had said the wrong word again.

Jake must have thought Luca said combat. "Foreigners," Jake said, shaking his head. He turned abruptly and ran a few steps to catch up with the others.

Luca felt terrible. Now all his classmates would know that he hadn't taken part in the defense of the city. That might have gone without notice in all the confusion of the day, if he hadn't met Jake. Luca resolved that next time the Militia Reserves were called up, he would go.

Chapter 18

Facing Facts

There was a loud rap on their door. Luca was surprised. Since they had come to Petersburg, few people had visited them. It was Saturday, four days after the excitement of May 5 and the preparations for the battle that never occurred. Ree was cleaning in the hallway and went to the door.

"I'm here to see Mrs. Streetman," a man said. Luca recognized his grandfather's voice.

"This way," said Ree. "I'll take your hat. Have a seat in the parlor. I'll fetch the missus."

Luca had been working on his weekly letter to his father. He put down the pen, put the cap on the ink bottle, and blotted the letter before going into the parlor.

His grandfather stood in front of the fireplace. Luca thought Gran looked worn down like the threshold in an old house. "Boy, I'm here to see your mother. I'm just back from spending the last four nights in the field with the Militia Reserves. And what I have to tell her, I'd just as soon you heard."

"Yes, sir." Luca brushed his hair from his forehead. There was a lot he wanted to ask his grandfather about the last few days, but he didn't know where to begin. Before he had a chance to formulate a question, his mother came into the parlor from the kitchen.

"Good morning, Luke," she said in her usual pleasant manner. "Won't you have a seat?" It seemed strange to hear Gran called Luke. It was his name, but Luca was used to thinking of him only as Gran.

"After you, Angelica," said Gran, with a slight bow. Luca's mother seated herself on the brown sofa. Gran took a chair facing her. Luca didn't know whether to stand or sit. His mother nodded, indicating that he should sit next to her.

"To what do I owe the pleasure of your visit?" Madre said with a directness unusual for her.

"As I'm sure you know, when a large Union army landed at City Point on Tuesday, everyone thought there would be an attack on Petersburg. More Federal troops are arriving every day." Gran paused for a moment and then continued. "Although Tuesday was a false alarm, the Union army will advance on Petersburg. It's only a matter of time."

"I've heard about the buildup of Union troops. I can only hope the war will be over before the city is attacked."

"The war won't be over until Petersburg falls. And I've been giving your situation a lot of thought. I didn't sleep well at Battery 5. My old bones don't much take to camping out anymore. I had a lot of time to think."

"What is our situation?"

"If or when the city falls, you'll be defenseless. Now, I know that Yankees don't make war on women and children, or so I've heard. But I also know soldiers. Sometimes soldiers get out of control, and then..." Gran's voice trailed off as if he were contemplating the awful things that might happen to an unprotected woman.

"I'm quite able to take care of myself," Madre said, sitting up taller.

"I'm sure you are, Angelica. But I promised my son that I'd look out for you and the boy. Now, you could move in with my tribe. But I didn't think you'd want to do that. I finally decided what would be the best solution."

"What do you propose?"

"I'm showing the boy how to use a gun. And I intend to give him one of mine."

"But Luca's only twelve. He's too young..."

"Angelica, boys in Virginia commonly learn how to shoot about at his age or younger. The boy's father shot his first deer when he was eleven."

"Shooting deer's not the same as...as...shooting people. I will not have a gun in this house. I will not condone violence."

"No one's asking you to." Gran's tone was grave. "The boy can keep the gun in the toolshed. I know you've got a shed out back. And he'll only use it if someone threatens you. Only if you're in danger."

"In Italy men are fighting to become united. And here, you are doing just the opposite. It makes no sense. Northerners and Southerners are very different in Italy, but we want to be one country. Everyone honors Garibaldi for sacrificing his conquests for national unity," his mother spoke calmly, but Luca could tell from her tone of voice that she was upset. "I don't understand you Americans. I don't approve of this war."

"I can't say I much like this war, or any war, for that matter. One of the reasons I sent Lawrence to school up north and encouraged him to enter the diplomatic service was that I've known for years that this war was coming. Frankly, Angelica, I didn't want him in it."

"I applaud the consideration you have shown my husband. Yet if you truly feel that way, how can you possibly consider arming Luca?"

"I don't like the idea of giving a gun to a boy who is as green as pond scum in summer, but sometimes you have to defend yourself. Sometimes there's no other reasonable alternative."

Madre's eyes filled with tears. Gran stood to leave. "Begging your pardon, Angelica, I better leave. Your tears may work on me. But I can't guarantee they'll work on drunken Yankees out to do mischief."

Gran headed for the door. Luca and his mother followed. "Boy, come with me. There's no time like the present." He picked up his hat from where Ree had hung it on the oak coatrack in the hall.

Luca looked at his mother. She wiped her eyes with a handkerchief and gave him her permission to leave with a slight nod of her head.

Once they were outside, Gran said, "I'm glad we've cleared the air over this gun business. I don't like sneaking around. Don't let me catch you ever sneaking around." He looked at Luca and his eyes narrowed. Luca guessed that Gran had seen him behind the tree at the Jordan farm. He felt the color rise in his cheeks. It seemed he couldn't do anything right.

Chapter 19

Boadicea

"Hey, Luca, wait up!" Jim called the next week after school. Ever since school had resumed, Luca had been avoiding Jim and the other boys. No one had said anything, but Luca sometimes felt that the word *coward* was written in big letters on his forehead. He half-wished somebody would say something. If some boy called him a coward, he'd fight him. That would prove he wasn't afraid.

"Luca!" Jim's voice was insistent. "Wait up!"

Luca stopped and turned to confront Jim. "Where have you been?" Jim asked as he came up to Luca.

"My grandfather has gotten serious about teaching me to shoot. I meet him now most days after school."

"That's good," said Jim. "Which way are you going?" Luca pointed toward the center of town. "I'll walk a way with you, if you don't mind."

"I don't mind," Luca said, and Jim fell into step beside him. They walked for a while in silence.

"Well, how's it going?"

"My grandfather's a stickler for doing everything methodically and precisely. He gets pretty impatient with me."

"Emmy's been asking after you. She's been wondering why you haven't stopped by lately."

"Tell her I've been busy." Luca was finding it hard to talk. He felt that his failure to accompany Jim and the other boys to Battery 5 stood between them like a giant iceberg. Jim, however, seemed unfazed by all that had happened. He seemed perfectly willing to go on as before, but Luca felt the need to say something. "I wasn't afraid to go with you and the others last Tuesday."

"Who says you were afraid?" asked Jim, obviously surprised at Luca's comment.

"You know how they are, Jake, Ben, and the others."

"Have they said anything?"

"Not yet, but I know what they think of me."

"Does it matter what they think of you?"

"Of course it matters. You wouldn't understand."

Jim laughed a bitter laugh. "You're right about that. Let's forget about them. Tell me if you've found out anything else about Eli."

Luca was glad to change the subject. He told Jim about following Eli to the clearing and seeing him hide the pouch.

"It's perfect," said Jim as they neared the bank on Bollingbrook Street where Luca was to meet his grandfather.

"What's perfect?" asked Luca. He was still curious about all the peculiar things he had observed with Eli.

"That shack belongs to Boadicea. She's a witch. At least some people *think* she is a witch. And Miss Maizie's Sara has been dabbling in voodoo for years.

Let's say that Eli is a Union spy, and he wanted to get messages to the Federal troops. No one would think a thing about him visiting Boadicea."

"But he didn't visit her. He never went near the shack."

"You said he had a basket with onions in it. I'll bet bringing onions to the old lady was a cover. A cover that he didn't need to use."

"Do you think there's a spy ring?"

"I don't know about that. But people are so used to peculiar things going on around Miss Maizie's that they have stopped paying Eli, Sara, and Miss Maizie any real mind. It takes someone like you, someone new here, to notice things like the fact that Eli always seems to be around when something's happening."

"I'm sorry I didn't stay to see if anyone came for the pouch. I could have at least looked in it."

"Maybe we could go out there on Saturday," suggested Jim. "The pouch may still be in the woodpile."

"All right. But I'm not very good at sneaking about. My grandfather spotted me out at the Jordan farm."

They were nearing Farmers Bank. "Let's meet Saturday afternoon. We might just find proof that Eli really is a spy."

"It'll probably be a waste of time, but it can't hurt anything. I've got to go. My grandfather will be waiting. I'll come by your aunt's house at two."

Chapter 20

The Hospital

"I want you to come to the Confederate States Hospital with me this morning," Madre said on Saturday. Ever since his grandfather's visit, Luca's mother had seemed sad and withdrawn. He had been extra careful when he was around her. Luca was afraid that she would burst into tears at any moment.

"I've promised Jim I'd meet him at two," Luca said.

"What I've got to show you won't take long."

"I'll be finished with this letter to father in a minute. Then I'll be ready to go." Luca added a few lines to the page he had written and put down the pen.

Madre was waiting for him in the kitchen. She was spending long hours at the hospital and she carried her lunch in a basket and usually included something special in it for the patients. Luca picked up the basket.

"It's a pretty morning," Luca said, as they made their way toward the hospital. Birds sang and chirruped. The new tree leaves were a brilliant spring green.

"It is nice," Madre said as they neared the main entrance of a building that had once been a warehouse.

"So nice, I dread going inside." She looked at Luca and smiled wistfully as they entered the hospital.

Luca's nose was immediately affronted with the overpowering smell of ether and carbolic. There were other smells too, the acrid smell of urine, and the rotten odor of decaying flesh. They entered a large room with exposed rafters and row upon row of cots. Every cot held a wounded soldier.

Two orderlies walked by carrying a stretcher. The man on it was completely covered with a sheet. Luca realized with a jolt that the man had died and was being carried out.

A woman in a white apron sat on a small stool beside a soldier, writing a letter. The eyes of the man

Confederate States Hospital in Petersburg
Courtesy of Petersburg National Battlefield

in the bed were bandaged. Luca watched one frail-looking woman walking among the beds carrying a heavy pail and dipper. She gave each soldier a drink. Luca wondered where the woman got the strength to continue.

Madre put down her basket and took out a clean apron. She said nothing to Luca. She approached a desk where a haggard man in a blood-stained, white shirt sat writing. The man looked up. "Doctor Jenkins, this is my son, Luca. I want to show him around," she said.

"That's fine, Mrs. Streetman," Doctor Jenkins said. "As soon as you're done, Mrs. Harrison needs someone to relieve her. She's been here most of the night." He bent again over his papers.

"This is the main ward," Madre said as she directed Luca along the row of beds. He tried not to stare at the

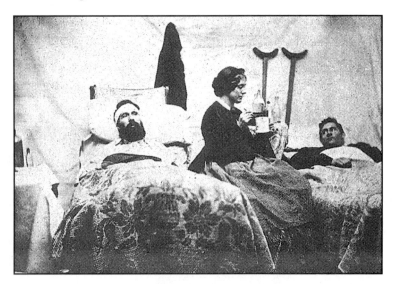

A nurse with wounded soldiers

U.S.A.M.I. Archival Group: Mollus-Mass, p. 3921

men in the beds as they passed. Most wore bloody bandages and were deathly pale. One man babbled incoherently. Another man kept calling, "Mother, Mother, why don't you help me?" Luca began to feel sick to his stomach.

They went down a corridor with cots all along it. A patient in one of the cots called out to Madre. He was just a boy, not much older than Luca, and tears streamed down his face. "Please, ma'am, please help me."

Madre stopped and went over to the boy. "What can I do for you, soldier?" Her voice was full of concern. She placed a hand on his forehead and then gently touched his cheek.

"I don't want to die," the boy said.

"You're not going to die," Madre said soothingly. "You'll start to feel better soon. It takes a while. I'll be back to see you later."

When Madre turned away, there were tears in her eyes. Luca followed her into another big, open room that was also full of beds. The patients in this part of the hospital were in better condition than the ones in the first room. Some were propped up with pillows. A few hobbled about. Most sported bloody bandages. A number were missing either an arm or a leg. One man was missing both legs.

Luca began to feel lightheaded, and he wondered if he was going to faint. He had seen amputees in town, but the sight of so many in one room was overwhelming. The hospital reminded him of the preacher's descriptions of damned souls in hell. The amputees seemed every bit as pitiful and forsaken as the sinners suffering eternal torment.

Madre didn't look at Luca. She smiled and greeted the patients as she passed their beds. They came to a robust-looking older woman, dressed in black. She was in the process of changing the bandages that covered the stump of a man's arm. Luca gagged.

"Hello, Mrs. Harrison," Madre said, "I'm here to relieve you. I'll be back after I show my son out. I'll just be a minute." Mrs. Harrison glanced up and nodded to Madre before resuming her grisly task.

Madre led Luca to a side door, and he walked out into the May sunshine. "Now you know why I'm against fighting and this awful war," she said without emotion. She looked at him and smiled. "You're looking a little peaked."

"I'm all right," Luca assured her.

"I'll see you at suppertime then," said Madre, turning toward where she had left Mrs. Harrison.

Luca's visit to the hospital had been upsetting, and he thought about the boy in the corridor, wondering if he was going to die. He knew now why Madre had said so little about his grandfather's visit to their house. The hospital visit was her response. She didn't need to say anything when she could show him the terrible damage caused by guns.

Chapter 21

The Voodoo Pouch

"I'm not sure this is a good idea," Luca whispered as he and Jim made their way to a spot near Boadicea's cabin later that afternoon. When they neared the clearing, they hid behind the same derelict farm wagon where Luca had concealed himself when he had spied on Eli.

They peered around the wagon. "That's Boadicea in front of her shack, hanging out laundry," Jim said into Luca's ear.

They watched as Boadicea hung the wet clothes on the line strung between two trees.

"She doesn't look all that scary to me," Luca whispered.

"Up close she's worse. Runny eyes and scars on her face."

"Let's play rock, paper, scissors while we're waiting."

The boys quietly played the game for a few minutes. The old woman moved slowly, and it seemed like it took her a very long time to finish hanging the wash. She finally put away her wash tub and went inside.

"We better wait a few minutes longer," said Jim. "If we get proof that Eli is a spy, what should we do next?"

"I'll talk to my grandfather. He'll know what to do."

"How are you two getting along?"

"All right, I guess. He's short with everybody except the ladies. He expects the Yankee attack will be sometime soon."

Jim and Luca fell silent. The fine morning had given way to a cloudy afternoon, and the humidity became oppressive. Mosquitoes buzzed around their heads, tormenting them.

"I've had enough," said Luca, as he slapped two mosquitoes in rapid succession.

"Me, too."

"This is pretty stupid. My mother has always said that I have a vivid imagination. I'm beginning to wonder if I haven't imagined this whole business. Let's make a run for the woodpile and get this over with."

"What if Boadicea is watching?"

"She probably is. What of it? Who's she going to tell? What's more to the point, how's she going to catch us?"

Luca stood and dashed toward the woodpile with Jim behind him. Luca went to the spot where he had seen Eli hide the pouch. He put his hand into the crevice between two logs and felt around. A moment later he pulled out the pouch. "Got it. Let's go!"

Jim and Luca ran toward the path. Luca cast a quick glance over his shoulder. He saw Boadicea in her window. His heart pounded violently in his chest.

When they reached the main road, Jim looked around. "This way." Jim led Luca through the trees to an abandoned tobacco shed.

They sat on the weathered doorstep. Luca opened the pouch and looked inside. It contained no letters or maps. Luca spilled the contents onto his hand. There were bones, six small, pointed teeth, and what appeared to be dried berries.

"Some spy," said Jim with disgust.

"What is this stuff?"

Jim examined the bones. "These are snake vertebrae. And these teeth belong to some kind of small animal. I'm not sure what." Jim examined the berry-like things. "I haven't a clue about these."

"What does it mean?"

"Count them."

"Six vertebrae, twelve seeds, and two berries. I think we've just stolen Eli's voodoo pouch. Boadicea will probably put a spell on us."

"Let me see it." Jim took the pouch from Luca and carefully examined it. "It seems you overlooked something." He removed a small square of folded brown paper, no bigger than a postage stamp. He carefully opened it. A trapezoid was drawn on it. Three lines bisected the trapezoid. One spot was marked with an X. He handed the paper to Luca.

"I'm sure Eli's up to something," said Luca.

"Black magic undoubtedly."

"Everyone, but everyone in Petersburg says that Eli is smart. How can a smart person believe in this voodoo mumbo jumbo?"

"It beats me. What are we going to do with this stuff now?"

"Let's return it to where we found it," said Luca. "I'm uneasy taking something that doesn't belong to me. Even this worthless junk. I feel kind of foolish, thinking I might prove Eli was a spy."

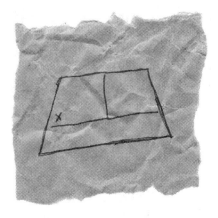

Small square of brown paper (magnified)

By the Author

They retraced their steps to the clearing and to the old wagon. Boadicea was no longer at her window, and after looking around cautiously, the boys dashed to the woodpile, and Luca thrust the pouch back where he had found it.

They jogged down the path that led to the main road. They had only gone a little way when Boadicea stepped out of the woods directly in front of them.

Startled, Luca and Jim stopped abruptly. The old woman glared at them with milky eyes. Her mouth opened in a gummy grimace. "What do you want?" she asked in a voice that sounded like the cackling of an old hen.

"Er, ah...*vorremo*...," Luca blurted out before he could stop himself. Boadicea's rummy eyes narrowed to slits. "I mean...we were just leaving."

"We've just been playing around," said Jim. "We didn't mean any harm."

"Stay away from my cabin," said Boadicea. Each word seemed to have a barb attached to it. She slowly stepped aside. Luca and Jim hurried by her. They felt her eyes on their backs as they walked to the road.

"Whew," said Luca, "I'd hate to meet her on a dark night."

"I can't say I much care for meeting her during the day," said Jim.

By the time they reached Jim's aunt's house, it was late afternoon, and Luca felt tired and out of sorts. Jim's aunt and mother were on the porch, and Luca forced himself to exchange the obligatory pleasantries with them for a few minutes. He was glad when he could leave and make his way toward home. He was only yards away when he heard a blood-chilling scream come from the back of the house.

Chapter 22

The Pig's Head

Luca ran inside and almost collided with Ree. Her apron was over her head and she was screeching at the top of her lungs. "They're going to get me! They're going to get me!"

Ree ran out the front door and Luca went after her. "What's the matter, Ree?" he asked when he caught up with her.

"I'm never coming back here!" she said in a hysterical voice. "They're going to get me!"

"Who's after you?" Luca put a steadying hand on the shaking woman.

"The spirits." Ree began walking away as they talked. "The spirits done visited. They've left a message. I'm not coming back!"

"Did you see anyone?"

"I didn't need to! I felt them. They've been here. They've left a message in the kitchen. I got to go." She shook free from Luca's steadying hand and hurried away.

Luca went into the house and headed to the kitchen. On the kitchen table was a suckling pig's head. There were sharpened sticks stuck in both eyes.

By the time his mother came home, Luca had removed the pig's head. He told his mother about his encounter with Ree and the pig's head. He did not tell her about his trip to Boadicea's clearing. "Where do you think it came from?" he asked.

"Some prank. Maybe those boys you pelted with eggs were getting even." Madre gave him a wry look.

Luca squirmed. "How did you know about the eggs?"

"A little bird told me," said Madre with the trace of a smile on her lips. "This is a very small town. I hope the pig's head is a prank. If so, it's a pretty nasty one. The thing that really bothers me is that someone came into our home. It makes me wonder if we're safe here."

"The kitchen door isn't far from the garden gate," Luca said, relieved that she wasn't going to pursue the business with the eggs. "It wouldn't take more than a couple of minutes for someone to slip into the kitchen and out again. I think we better start locking our doors."

"I don't think Ree will be back," Luca said.

"It may be just as well. Things are growing so expensive in town I'm not sure we can afford her anyway." His mother sank tiredly into a chair. "At times like this, a spotlessly clean house doesn't seem all that important."

Luca wondered whom he could ask about the pig. Then it came to him. "When does Jordan come again?"

"He's coming tomorrow afternoon to weed and water. I don't much like him coming on Sunday. But I'm glad with all the work in town these days that he'll come at all."

"Are we invited out for dinner tomorrow?"

"I saw Mrs. S. yesterday at the hospital. She was delivering bandages made by her sewing circle. She invited us to Sunday dinner. I declined." Madre put her feet up on the little step stool near her chair. "I'm too tired these days to make polite conversation."

That night, Madre locked the doors before turning in. Luca was tired. It had been quite a day, but once he was settled in his bedroom under the eaves of the old house, he couldn't sleep.

Rain began to fall. Luca listened for a long time to the soft patter on the window, trying to piece together the events of the afternoon. What did the stuff in the pouch mean? Was it something for a spell or a curse? He tossed and turned, getting tangled in the bed sheets. He thought about the pig's head. What was that all about? Was it from Boadicea? If it was some sort of voodoo revenge for taking the pouch, how did Boadicea manage to get the pig's head to his house before he arrived home? The whole business with the pig's head made him feel vulnerable, violated, as if someone was watching him take a bath. And what was going on at Miss Maizie's? Was the old lady somehow caught up in whatever Eli was doing? It all made his head spin.

The rain grew heavier and the patter was replaced by an insistent drumming sound. Maybe Madre was right, maybe the pig's head was a prank played by Freddie Purdy and Creepy Eddie. He hadn't been bothered by them since they had tied him up. Perhaps they felt that they hadn't settled their score with him. It was all very confusing. He needed to talk with Jordan. With this thought in mind, he finally drifted into sleep.

The next afternoon Luca waited eagerly for Jordan. It was nearly five o'clock when Jordan ambled up the walk. "Howdy," he said.

"Howdy yourself,"said Luca. He finished loosening the soil around a struggling pepper plant and stood. "I've got something to show you before we begin work. Ree was scared of it. I know you won't be. I'm depending on you to tell me what it's all about."

"What you got?" said Jordan with curiosity.

Luca led Jordan to the place behind a dogwood tree where he had put the pig's head. He peered into the tall grass. "It's gone!"

"What's gone?"

"A pig's head with stakes in its eyes. Ree found it on our kitchen table."

Luca had never realized before that dark-skinned people became pale, but he watched as Jordan seemed to lose his healthy, rosy-brown hue.

"What does it mean?" Luca asked.

"It means somebody's going to...," Jordan swallowed hard and continued, "to die."

Chapter 23

Learning to Shoot

"I've been thinking about the stuff in that pouch," Jim said, Monday after school. He seemed excited, and Luca hadn't had a chance yet to tell him about the pig's head. "I wonder if those things are some sort of a code. What if the snake vertebrae, for example, referred to the number of regiments in town or something like that."

"I hadn't thought of that," said Luca. "How would we find out?"

"I don't know. But when I want to find something out, I always go to the library. I know the librarian there. Old Mr. Jarvis is a walking encyclopedia. And if he doesn't know something, or can't find it out for you, he takes it as some kind of professional or personal failure."

"What will you ask him? You can't tell him about us snatching the pouch."

"But I can ask him about voodoo. Somebody surely has written a book about it. Maybe a book would tell us what the stuff we found means."

"While you're looking it up, you might find out what a pig's head means." Luca told Jim about finding the pig's head on the kitchen table and what Jordan had said about it.

Jim's eyes grew large and his jaw dropped. "I don't like all this. And I'm not sure what I'll find out."

"What do you hope to find out?"

"Let's say that what we found in the pouch is a voodoo love charm. Then we know we've been off track. On the other hand, if the stuff doesn't mean anything in the voodoo religion, then it might represent something like the locations and dispositions of the Confederate troops."

"Want me to go to the library with you?"

"Aren't you meeting your grandfather?"

"Yes, we're having target practice in a little while."

"Well then, maybe you can find out from your grandfather about the manning of the fortifications. That seems to me to be the key thing that the Union generals would want to know."

"I'll try. But I never know about my grandfather. Sometimes he will talk with me. Other times he's impatient and cross as if I were just another of the many burdens he must bear."

"A lot of adults are like that. See what you can find out, and I'll go to the library. I'll come by your house after dinner and we'll compare notes." Jim hurried off in the direction of the library. Luca turned toward his grandfather's bank.

"Boy," Gran said as Luca neared Farmers Bank, "you're late. And we need to get at it since I've got a meeting with Major Archer and the Militia Reserves at five."

"I'm sorry, Gran," said Luca. The afternoon was not starting off well.

Gran had two rifles with him today and a bag of bottles. "This is a Mississippi rifle." He showed Luca a well-cared-for gun. "It's from the Mexican War. I brought it along just so you could see it. I might take a shot or two myself. It was given to me by Jeff Davis years ago when he headed up the Mississippi volunteers."

"Is that the same Jefferson Davis who's now president of the Confederacy?"

Model 1841 U.S. percussion rifle, AKA "Mississippi rifle," Robbins and Lawrence, Windsor, Vt., c. 1850

Courtesy of the Virginia War Museum, Newport News, Va.

"It surely is the same fellow. It's my favorite rifle and one of my most prized possessions. You'll have to use this other one."

Gran gave Luca the other gun, the one Luca would use for target practice. Luca held it loosely as they walked toward the farm where Gran had arranged for them to have target practice.

"Don't swing that gun around," Gran said with irritation. "It's not a toy."

Luca rested the heavy gun in the crook of his arm. He tried to think how he might broach the subject of the number and disposition of troops guarding the city. Gran seemed distant, preoccupied.

"Gran," he ventured, "why aren't there troops available to guard Petersburg?"

Gran seemed to come back from some place far away. "We're really short of men. Part of the reason is that Petersburg has sent seventeen separate units to the war. Some people say that more Petersburg men are fighting for the Confederacy than there are registered voters in the city."

"Well, we've got the Militia Reserves, haven't we?"

"Yes, but we're not really a military force. You saw what we looked like. Out-of-date guns, no uniforms, little or no training. The Militia Reserves with all its last-minute volunteers is a poor excuse for a military unit. I say that even though I'm a member of it."

Gran took out his pipe. He paused for a moment while he filled it and took his first puff. Luca thought Gran seemed to be warming to the discussion. "Why isn't General Lee's army defending us?" Luca asked.

"General Lee's been pretty busy over in the Wilderness. There's been a big battle, and a lot of casualties have come to the hospitals here."

"How many men are defending the city?" Luca hoped that he was not making Gran suspicious by asking too many questions.

"About twelve hundred," said Gran, "counting the Militia Reserves. We've only got two regular military units and a few field guns."

"Could the Union army easily take the city?"

"They greatly outnumber us. However, at this point, it's not clear they know how thin our troops are spread behind the Dimmock Line. It's a wonder they haven't advanced on Petersburg before now. Now you know why I'm concerned. Why I'm teaching you to shoot."

When they arrived at the farm, they went in back of the barn. Gran set up two bottles on the split-rail fence. "Boy, I want you to load as rapidly as you can and shoot until you've hit those two bottles. You need to concentrate. Make each shot count."

Luca tore open the paper cartridge, and he fumbled as he trickled the powder into the muzzle of the gun. "Boy!" his grandfather bellowed. "Be calm!"

Luca wadded the paper and put it into the muzzle. His fingers felt like they were as big as piano keys as he put in the minié ball and rammed it down into the muzzle. He aimed and carefully detonated the percussion cap, trying to remember accurately the steps his grandfather had taught him. The loud report of the shot startled Luca and the heavy gun kicked like a mule and bruised his shoulder. The bottles still stood on the fence.

"Again," said Gran, "faster this time!" He was becoming more and more irritable. "We're not getting ready for a tea party. You have to be able to load, aim, and fire without thinking."

Luca began to sweat. He fired the gun again and again. And still the bottles stood on the fence.

"That's enough," Gran said, shaking his head as though Luca was completely hopeless. "I have to go. Take the gun home with you. Don't let your mother see it. There's no point in pulling a cat's tail unless you want to get scratched. We'll do this again tomorrow."

Luca could tell that his performance had not pleased his grandfather, but he didn't know what to say.

"I'd quite forgotten how long it takes to learn how to do anything well," said Gran. His lined face was grave. "The only problem is that right now we don't have a lot of time."

Chapter 24

In Miss Maizie's Garden

Luca heard three loud and then three soft raps on the door. He had told his mother that Jim was coming over, and they were going outside for a while. They had just finished eating supper, and he was helping her clear the table. "That must be Jim," he said.

"You go along," Madre said. "I'll finish up here."

Luca grabbed his box of toy soldiers from the table near the front door. Luca thought Jim would enjoy seeing them since he knew so much about military history. They could look at the soldiers after they talked. Luca joined Jim outside in the warm spring evening.

"What did you find out?" asked Luca as they walked toward the center of town.

"I learned a lot. I studied a great book about charms and potions. There was even a table that listed things like rabbit's feet and what they meant in the voodoo religion. I didn't find a pig's head. But I did verify that you can put a curse on someone by sticking a pin or a sharp object into a representation of them."

"It's confusing. Miss Maizie said that Pat didn't have a face so that a child could pretend the doll was different people. Do you suppose Miss Maizie uses Pat to put curses on someone? Someone like a troublesome neighbor?"

"It seems rather far-fetched to me. It's hard to imagine Miss Maizie wishing anyone ill. But then again, the whole voodoo business is kind of crazy."

"Did you find out what the things in the pouch mean?"

"I found out they're not voodoo objects. If they have any meaning, it's not one that is commonly associated with voodoo practices."

The street was still bright with the slanting rays of the setting sun. "Twelve seeds," said Luca, thinking out loud. "I asked my grandfather about the defenses. He said there were about twelve hundred men available to defend the city. What if the twelve seeds meant the twelve hundred men?"

"If that's the case, what could the vertebrae mean?"

Luca thought for a moment, trying to remember the conversation with his grandfather. He pushed his hair off his forehead. "Gran said something about guns. I think he said that we had only a few field guns. What if there were six guns?"

"And the two berries? I looked them up in a botany book. They're dried pokeberries."

"Gran said that we had two regular military units. Could that explain the berries?" Luca and Jim exchanged looks.

"I don't know. But tomorrow I'm going to try and find out exactly how many field guns we have," said Jim.

"How will you find out?"

"I'm not sure."

"What about the little piece of paper with the trapezoid on it?"

"I'm convinced it means the Trapezium House. What else could it be? The X must indicate where something is hidden. You do know Miss Maizie owns the Trapezium House and no one has lived in it for a long time."

"I knew it was vacant, but I didn't know Miss Maizie owned it."

"Miss Maizie's mother was a sister of the man who built it, or so I've heard. According to some people, that's one reason she's crazy."

"What do you mean?"

"Well, the Trapezium House is so...so off balance. People think it is cursed."

"I see," said Luca, not really sure that he understood at all. He made a mental note to ask Gran about Miss Maizie when he had the chance.

"By the way, did you know that Jordan is Boadicea's grandson?"

"This place never ceases to amaze me. Everyone's related or connected in some way or another. And gossip flies around this town as fast as a hummingbird. Do you want to see my soldiers?"

"Of course," said Jim, his face brightening.

They sat on the steps of St. Paul's Episcopal Church, and Luca opened the wooden box.

Luca began taking out the soldiers. Jim picked one up. "They're wonderful," Jim said. "You even have the Coldstream Guards!"

"Here, look at this one." Luca handed Jim an impressive soldier on a prancing white horse.

"Whew," whistled Jim in admiration, "Napoleon himself."

"It's too bad we're too grown up to play soldiers."

"You may be too grown up, but I'm not. Let's stage a battle." Jim began to position the soldiers on the steps.

"French or English?" asked Luca. "You choose."

"How could I pass up having Napoleon lead my army?" Jim picked up the famous general and set him down in front of the French soldiers.

The battle raged until the light faded and the soldiers almost became indistinguishable from the gray stone steps. "I think we better call it a day," said Jim, edging his soldiers back from the lines of battle. "Army retreat!"

Luca marched his soldiers—even the ones who had fallen in battle—one by one into the box, and Jim followed suit.

"Let's go by Miss Maizie's house," said Luca.

"What for?" asked Jim, as they began to walk in the direction of her house.

"No particular reason, just that there's something strange going on there."

"That's nothing new," Jim said. "Most people stay away from the place. They've stayed away from it for at least forty years."

"I wish you could do some research and find out what's really been going on at Miss Maizie's."

"It's not the kind of thing you find in the library."

"But somebody must know. I bet Gran knows."

"You've learned how people in Petersburg gossip. If anybody knew anything, it would be all over town."

"Not necessarily," said Luca, thinking that the incident with the leeches had not created a stir because he had not said anything about it.

It was almost dark as they neared Miss Maizie's. A light was on in the parlor, the parlor where Pat sat in her little chair. They walked by the house to the side gate. They looked over the fence into the garden. They were about to cross the street and go home when the back door opened and Eli came out with a lantern.

Luca grabbed Jim by the sleeve, and they crouched beside the fence. They peered through the narrow slats at Eli. He began digging with a shovel. He dug for a while and then put something into the hole and covered it.

"Could he be burying a pig's head?" Luca whispered.

Before Jim could answer, Eli went to the back door and led Miss Maizie outside.

"I thought she never went outside," whispered Jim.

"Eli told us she usually doesn't go outside."

Miss Maizie stood for a while next to Eli. They spoke in low voices, but Jim and Luca were too far away to hear what they said. Then Eli took Miss Maizie's arm and led her back inside.

Jim and Luca waited for a few minutes before they crossed the street and headed home. "Do you suppose that Miss Maizie's involved with whatever Eli's doing?" asked Luca.

Jim thought for a minute. "I wouldn't have believed it before tonight. But now I don't know."

Old Street in downtown Petersburg
Courtesy of the Petersburg Museums, City of Petersburg

Chapter 25

Making Plans

It was raining on Wednesday after school. Jake Leighton and Ben McIlwaine stood in a huddle with their friends under the portico in front of the entrance to the school building.

Luca stood off to one side. "Let's all go to my house," Jake said. "We can make plans from there." Luca watched as the boys walked by him. Neither Jake nor Ben had said one word to him since the Militia Reserves had been called out on May 5. Luca knew that they thought he was a coward, and as such, beneath their contempt. Just then, Jim appeared in the door.

"Hey, Jim," said Jake, "Want to join us?"

"No thanks," Jim said. He and Luca watched as the group, with Jake in the lead, took off in the direction of his house.

"I'm tired of this rain," said Luca. He had not seen Jim except in class since the week before.

"I'm tired of it, too, but not as tired as I am of Leighton and his ilk."

"What do you mean?"

"It's just that since the May 5 business, they have invited me a couple of times to join them."

"Why didn't you?" asked Luca, thinking that he would like nothing better than to join their clique.

"If you don't know, I'm not going to tell you." Jim looked at Luca for a moment as if he were some kind of half-wit.

"They are *the group* to belong to in Petersburg," Luca said defensively.

"Yeah, I suppose they are. If you want to belong to a group." Jim looked thoughtfully at Luca for a moment and then changed the subject. "Are you still doing your target practice?"

"Every day if it isn't pouring. I'm improving, but not fast enough for my grandfather. Because it's raining cats and dogs today, I'll have a chance to do something else for a change. Not that there's much anybody can do on a day like this."

"Can we go to your house? We need to talk. There's some sort of hospital auxiliary meeting going on at my aunt's."

"Sure," said Luca, "Madre's at the hospital, and she'll be there until supper time." Dodging the rain as best they could, the two boys ran toward Luca's house on High Street.

"I've found out about the field guns," Jim said when they were inside and seated comfortably in the kitchen, having some of Madre's good bread and strawberry jam. "With Union soldiers only a few miles away, I decided it was too risky to ask around. I didn't want anyone thinking I was a spy. So, I went out and counted them."

"It's a ten-mile walk around the Dimmock line. You told me so yourself."

"I didn't have anything else to do, and I didn't do it all in one day."

"How many field guns are there?"

"Six. And I learned yesterday that the Militia Reserves are being moved to Battery 12. It could be that the twelve seeds stood for that."

"I thought Battery 5 was crucial. Why were they moved?"

"I'm not sure. I have heard they are moving again to Battery 27 where the Jerusalem Plank Road comes into the Dimmock Line."

"Would Eli give this kind of information to the Yankees?"

"I don't know if the bluecoats are interested in the whereabouts of such a ragtag bunch as the Militia Reserves."

"Unless the Federals want to attack wherever the Militia Reserves are stationed. Is it giving the Union generals too much credit to think they might want to attack the weakest link in our defenses?"

"Probably," Jim said.

"What should we do about Eli?"

"Imagine telling an adult we stole the pouch that Eli left at Boadicea's place," Jim said. "And the snake vertebrae, seeds, and berries are really a coded message to the Union soldiers. No one will believe us. We need proof. Let's go look at the Trapezium House. I'm convinced there's something going on there. People swear they've seen lights upstairs. The rain is easing off and we've got time before supper."

Luca and Jim headed down the hill toward Market Street. Scattered drops of rain still fell, but the sky was clearing to the East. The air smelled as fresh as clean laundry. The street was muddy, and they leapt across puddles and tried to avoid the squishy ruts in the road.

"Do you suppose there's a spy ring operating in town?" Luca asked, when they reached a brick sidewalk and were able to talk again.

"I didn't think so before, but I do now. How can there help but be? Every slave is a potential spy. Why should slaves be loyal to the Confederacy when they can be free if they reach Union lines? It's to their advantage to help the Union cause in any way possible. I think Eli's smart. He's using voodoo as a smoke screen, and it works. It works so well that no one would believe us if we went to them with the story about the pouch."

They neared the Trapezium House. "This place is scary, even in the daytime," Luca said, as he studied the lopsided house with its shutters all closed. "I'm not sure I'd like going inside it."

"I'd love to go inside," Jim said, pausing for a moment to study the house. "I've always been curious about the floor plan. Imagine, no square or rectangular rooms. I have a feeling that it just might hold the proof we need."

They walked on by the house. "We've got to find a time to get inside when no one will see us," Luca said.

"It won't be easy."

Chapter 26

The Trapezium House

Luca met Jim on the corner in front of the Trapezium House. It was two days later, and it was growing dark. "Did your mother want to know where you were going?" Jim asked.

"She asked, and I said I was meeting you. I think she assumed that I was going to your house."

"I just left without telling anyone. That's one advantage of walking around with a book on your head occasionally. No one questions you. They just think you're doing something strange, but harmless," said Jim with a knowing grin. He showed Luca a lantern. "I got this from the barn."

"What if someone sees the light?"

"The shutters on the house are all closed. And we'll need it to see. We'll have to take the chance that if someone sees the light, they'll think it's ghosts or something."

"Do you really think Eli would be frightened of ghosts?" Luca laughed. The idea amused him.

"Let's just hope that Eli's busy somewhere else. We can't afford to wait. There's a lot of talk in town

Trapezium House

A trapezium is a four-sided figure without parallel sides. Thus, it has no right angles. When used in construction, the effect is slightly unsettling, as if the house were tilted or the observer a bit off balance. Charles O'Hara, according to local legend, was told by a trusted West Indian servant that evil spirits could not dwell in such a house. The house dates from 1817. At the time of this writing, it is privately owned.

about the Yankees. I heard Uncle Pete telling Mother that he expects an attack any day now."

They slipped through the gate that surrounded the small yard and snuck up to the back door. It was not quite fully dark yet, and in the fading light, Jim took a piece of wire from his pocket and began fiddling at the keyhole.

"Where did you learn to pick locks?"

"It's easy," Jim said, snapping open the lock and holding the door for Luca to enter the house. "My mother had a little chest with a broken lock, and I took it to the locksmith. I sat around and watched him work. He told me all about locks. He wouldn't have told Freddie and Eddie about them, but he knew I wouldn't be breaking into houses. Or so he thought..."

Luca followed Jim inside and shut the door. They were surrounded by blackness. Inside the house was a deeper, more menacing darkness than any darkness Luca had ever experienced. The house smelled of mildew and decay. Luca breathed the cold and damp in, and he felt like he had entered a long-unopened tomb.

Jim lit the lantern, turning it down to its lowest setting. Luca's eyes grew accustomed to the faint light, and he looked around. The whole first floor was one large room, filled with broken furniture, old trunks, and debris. He immediately felt disoriented, dizzy. Everything was off kilter, tilted, even the mantle over the fireplace. "This isn't the room that was marked on the paper," Jim said in a whisper.

"Why are you whispering?"

"The place makes me feel like I should," said Jim in a more normal tone. They both listened for a moment. The silence was so complete that it felt threatening.

"It's bizarre," Luca said, "I feel like someone's watching us."

"It's your imagination." Jim looked about as they crossed the room, making their way between boxes and trunks. "It's these crazy angles. This room is a long, narrow trapezoid." He held the lamp in a corner for a moment to examine the angle. "It makes you feel something's just not right."

"Let's go upstairs. Remember, the paper indicated two rooms." Luca headed up a steep, narrow staircase. Jim followed, walking carefully, as if he might lose his balance. The lantern cast strange shadows in the stairway. A floorboard creaked, and in the eery silence, it sounded like a gunshot. Startled, Luca and Jim stood still and listened, then went on. They entered a narrow hallway. There were two sets of double doorways on the right.

"Shall we see what's in here?" asked Jim, as they paused before the first set of doors.

"In the drawing, the X was in one corner of the trapezoid. So, it's probably the next set of doors."

"There are trapezoids within trapezoids. Whoever designed this place was crazy, off-balance, weird."

At the same time, both Luca and Jim saw movement in the hallway. They froze. The dim light revealed nothing, and the silence was as thick and oppressive as before. "What was that?" Jim asked.

"Let's find out." The two boys moved cautiously forward toward shadows that moved in the dim light.

As they drew nearer, Jim held up the light. They started to laugh. "I should have known there would be a mirror somewhere in the hall," he said.

Luca put his hand on the doorknob of the second set of doors. He turned the knob, the door swung open, and they went inside. Leather-bound books lined the walls from floor to ceiling. "This is great!" said Jim. "There are more books here than in the library." He went to the shelves and began examining the titles. He shook his head. "All this knowledge just going to waste. It's too bad."

"Look!" Luca pointed to a footprint in the dust on the hardwood floor at the edge of the India carpet. "Somebody's been here recently."

Jim tore himself away from the books to examine the footprint. "It could be Eli's. I'm sure he looks after this property for Miss Maizie."

"He's one big guy. I've never looked at his feet particularly, but I'd guess he has big feet. Whoever made this boot print had a small foot."

"I wish I knew what we're looking for," said Jim, as they slowly examined the room. There were several chairs covered with sheets and a big desk in one corner. It had no cover on it, and Jim and Luca walked over to it.

The desk looked ordinary enough, except that it, like the room, had no right angles. It too was trapezoid-shaped. Two tiny bright eyes shone in the lantern light.

Jim and Luca froze. A mouse scurried off the desk and with a skittering noise disappeared in the surrounding darkness. "I can't believe I was scared by a wee mousie," said Jim, going over to the desk. On it were the remains of a loaf of bread and an opened glass jar.

"Someone's been here recently."

Jim examined the jar, smelling of it. "Peaches," he said. Beside the jar was a stack of drawings and a rolled-up piece of paper. Jim picked up several drawings and studied them.

Luca carefully unrolled the piece of paper. "This is it! The proof we've been looking for. It's a map!"

Jim held the lantern so that they could see it more clearly. "It's the Dimmock Line and all the Confederate troop deployments. And these drawings appear to be for a repeating gun. Or at least that's what they look like." Jim showed Luca the drawings. "I bet this is what Henry Pate was working on at the foundry."

Jim put the drawings down and was just about to pick up another stack of papers when they heard a muffled noise. "Someone's coming!" said Jim, dousing the light.

"Come on!" Luca hastily put the map back where he had found it. He grabbed Jim's hand. Luca groped his way into the hall, dragging Jim behind him.

Luca felt for the next set of doors as he edged along in the blackness. He turned the knob and they entered the other room. A cobweb caught in his hair. He raised a hand and batted furiously at the silky strands, shuddering at the thought that there might be a spider in his hair.

Footsteps came down the hall and someone entered the front room. Had whoever it was seen a sliver of light from their lantern through the closed blinds? Or was someone coming for the map and the drawings?

The map! Luca didn't have it. He turned toward Jim. He cupped his hand around Jim's ear. "Do you have the drawings?"

Jim shook his head, and Luca hit his head with his hand. Why hadn't they taken the drawings and the map? That was the proof they needed! That would convince everyone that Eli was a spy!

"We've got to get out of here. We're near the stairs," whispered Jim.

"Come on!" Luca reacted instantly. He pulled open the door. He ran for the stairs with Jim at his heels.

"Out the front!" Jim called.

They bounded down the stairs to the front door, dimly lit from the fan-shaped window above it.

Luca fumbled with the lock. The man was right behind them.

Chapter 27

June 9

Luca threw open the door. "Separate!" he shouted. He ran in one direction while Jim took off in another.

Luca plunged into the darkness. He was headed away from the Trapezium House when he crashed into a dark figure lurking in the shadows.

Luca reeled. He was recovering his balance when a hand grabbed him. He saw Eli's massive form in the dim light from the streetlight in front of the Trapezium House. "Stay away from here, or you'll be sorry!" Eli shook Luca like a wolf shaking its prey.

Luca twisted free of Eli's grasp and ran. He tore through an alley and across a vacant field, gasping for breath. He didn't stop until he was sure no one was following. He circled around to Jim's house and found him on the front porch.

"He didn't follow me," said Jim, still out of breath. "And he apparently didn't follow you. I wonder why. Maybe he couldn't run or maybe he had better things to do."

"Whoever it was, he probably didn't want anyone to know he was in the Trapezium House. And would you believe I bumped into Eli, just outside?"

"I knew it. Eli has to be part of a spy ring."

"What should we do now?"

"We can't do anything else tonight. Let's discuss it tomorrow before school. If we'd gotten the map or the drawings, it would be a different matter. By now they're probably on their way to the Yankees."

The next morning Jim was waiting outside when Luca got to school. "I thought about it and thought about it. I'll just have to tell my grandfather everything when I see him today after school," said Luca.

"Will he believe you?"

"I don't know. I hope so."

The school bell rang. "I guess we've got to go in," said Luca. "It's too nice a day to be inside all day, especially when a meeting with Gran is hanging over my head."

"Even if he does believe you, your grandfather can't do anything without proof. Why didn't we take the map and the drawings?"

"I feel really stupid," said Luca as they hurried to their classroom.

"I do, too. I would have liked the chance to study the plans for the gun. I wonder how it's supposed to work."

Cadaver Barnum stood in the front of the room, reading the roll. He gave them a disapproving look as they took their seats, but he didn't say anything.

Luca took out his books. It was nine o'clock. Mr. Barnum called Jim's name. He answered, "Here."

At that moment, bells all over town began to peal. Nobody waited for Mr. Barnum to dismiss the class. Everyone knew what was happening. The boys rushed out of the classroom and raced toward Courthouse

Square. Mr. Barnum, the principal, and several of the other teachers followed the boys. All over town, people poured into the streets.

"The Yankees are coming!" someone shouted.

By the time Jim and Luca reached the courthouse, the word had spread. A large Union force was moving toward Petersburg on Jerusalem Plank Road. An officer of the militia stood on the steps of the courthouse. The crowd quieted as he began to speak. "Everyone who can carry a gun should go to Battery 27 to aid the Militia Reserves." Pandemonium broke out.

"I'm going to get my father's gun," said Jim, yelling above the commotion. "I hope this is another false alarm."

"I'll meet you at your aunt's house," said Luca, hurrying off in the direction of his house before Jim could reply.

All over town, boys and men, wearing their everyday clothes, scurried to get their weapons. Luca was glad that Madre was at the hospital. He knew she must have heard the alarm, but he doubted she would leave her post. He reached the toolshed in the garden and took the gun from behind the garden tools where he had stashed it. He stuffed the ammunition box into his pocket. He had the funny feeling that Madre was watching him. But when he stepped outside into the sunlight, he saw no one.

Luca ran most of the way to Jim's house and found him in the front yard with Emmy. Jim's mother, pale and drawn, stood on the porch with his aunt.

"Are you ready?" Luca asked as he joined Jim.

Jim nodded. "My uncle's already gone."

"I wish I could go too," said Emmy.

Luca knew how she felt. It was awful being left behind when the city was in danger. "You can do something for me," he said, "if you will."

"Of course," said Emmy.

"If we're not back by supper, will you go by my house on High Street and tell my mother where I am?"

"She doesn't know you're going with the others?"

Luca swallowed. "No, she wouldn't approve."

"All right," said Emmy. She frowned, and her serious face made Luca almost laugh.

"Thanks," Luca said.

"We better go," said Jim. He hastily said his goodbyes.

"Be careful," his mother said, wiping her eyes. "Both of you!"

"What now?" asked Luca, as they left the house.

"There's no point in going to Courthouse Square. Let's head in the direction of Battery 27. That's where everybody's going."

Luca was glad they weren't going to Courthouse Square. He still worried that Madre or Gran would see him, and it was probably best to avoid the center of town.

Luca and Jim joined the stream of civilians headed toward Battery 27. Women and girls watched and waved from windows and porches. "Are you going to get in trouble for going with us?" Jim asked.

"Probably, but Gran told me that sometimes you have to stand your ground and fight."

When they reached the Dimmock Line, no one seemed to be in charge. Everyone was talking at once.

Nobody seemed to be doing anything except standing around. Luca spotted Gran. He stood with the other older men, holding his Mississippi rifle.

Finally, Major Archer assembled the Militia Reserves. Although the men and boys had stopped talking, Jim and Luca, standing in the back, couldn't hear clearly what he said.

"Did you get any of that?" Jim asked after the major had finished.

"He said something about never yielding, and standing up for homes and firesides."

Major Archer gave orders that Luca couldn't hear. A group of men rushed to a farm wagon and dragged it to the middle of Jerusalem Plank Road. They turned it over with a loud crash. Then they ripped out fence rails and constructed a barricade around it. It looked pretty flimsy to Luca.

"You two, over here," said an officer, motioning to Jim and Luca. They followed the man to a low earthwork, on the right of Jerusalem Plank Road. "You're to hold this area along with the rest of the Junior Reserves." Luca saw Jake Leighton and his friends stationed with other young militiamen nearby.

Without another word, the officer left. The earthwork that Luca and Jim crouched behind was only waist high and in poor repair. Luca looked around. The terrain was flat, unlike the area around Battery 5. He could see two houses and outbuildings. He looked down the line. Old men and boys without uniforms, holding all kinds of odd weapons, were taking their places along it. He saw Gran standing behind the earthwork on the other side of the road, talking to several businessmen.

It seemed like a lot of militia had gathered, but once they were spread out along the earthworks and behind the battery, the line looked poorly defended. There were no regular soldiers anywhere in sight. Luca noted that there were seven gun ports in the battery. But they were empty.

Luca and Jim began loading their guns. With trembling hands, Luca carefully followed Gran's step-by-step instructions. Then they waited. Time passed slowly. "Let's count the Militia Reserves," said Luca after a while. "It'll help to pass the time."

"I don't think we can see them all from here, but we can get a pretty good idea how many men we have."

They took turns standing on top of the earthwork and counting. "There's over a hundred," said Jim, "about 125, I'd say."

"That's not very many. How many Union soldiers do you suppose there will be?"

"Lots, but they probably won't attack here."

Suddenly, two mounted Confederates galloped up Jerusalem Plank Road. They rode into Battery 27 shouting, "The Yankees! Right behind us!"

Luca strained his eyes and saw a line of blue-coated cavalry materialize in the distance in a cloud of dust. A moment later, he heard the thunder of horses, as they charged down Jerusalem Plank Road.

Chapter 28

Yankee Attack

"Stay down!" someone yelled at Luca. "Stay down! No one fire until Major Archer gives the signal!"

Luca squatted beside Jim. He could feel the blood pounding in his head. He eased up just enough to peek over the earthwork. A mass of blue-coated cavalry careened toward them, drawn sabers glittering in the morning sun. They advanced faster and faster as they neared the line. Then they were only yards away.

"Fire!" came the command. Luca fired with the others; as he did so, he heard Jim's gun explode.

Luca turned. Jim lay on the ground, writhing in pain. The whole side of his face was bloody and blackened. Luca dropped his gun and went to his friend's side. A cavalryman and his horse had fallen right in front of Battery 27, and Luca heard the screams of the dying horse.

"Jim, get up!" he cried. "You've got to get out of here!" He helped Jim to his knees.

"My glasses are gone...and I've burned my hands." Jim looked down in shock and amazement at his bloody and blackened hands.

"You've got to get to a doctor!" yelled Luca. No one had told them where to go, or what to do, if they were hurt.

"Get back to your gun!" Jim screamed. "They're almost on us!"

Luca picked up his gun amid the crack and snap of rifle fire. In front of Battery 27, horses reared and plunged. A Union officer was barking out commands, but Luca couldn't hear his words over the shouts of the men. Luca reloaded rapidly, his fingers remembering his grandfather's careful instructions and the hours of practice. He glanced over at Jim just in time to see him get to his feet and run off.

Luca had no time to think—too much was happening too quickly. He aimed, fired, reloaded, and fired again. It was as if he were a gear in a big mechanical clock. Clouds of burned powder hung in the air, stinging his eyes. He aimed and hoped his shots helped to turn back the advancing army. He was ready to fire again when the blue-coated horde began to retreat. Luca lowered his gun. It was then he realized he was shaking all over.

A cheer went up from the Militia Reserves. A young blacksmith from the foundry climbed up on top of the earthworks. He waved his coat at the retreating Federals and cried, "Try it again! Try it again, if you dare!"

Luca stood up. He had to find Jim. Where had he gone? Jim needed medical help. Luca looked around, trying to remember exactly where Jim had disappeared. Luca saw his grandfather talking to Major Archer. At the same moment, Gran spotted him. Gran paused in his conversation and glared at him. With a movement of his hand, he signaled for Luca to wait.

Luca reloaded his gun, thinking about Jim. Gran finished his business with Major Archer and came to where Luca stood behind the earthwork.

"Boy, what are you doing here?" yelled Gran. His face was red, and he was shaking his fist at Luca.

"I had to come, Gran." Luca looked down at his feet.

"Your mother will have my hide for this. She'll be as angry as a polecat with a knot in its tail."

"Jim's been hurt, sir." Luca's words rushed out. "His gun exploded. It's my fault. We practiced every day, and Jim never practiced. I don't think he ever even shot that old gun from the War of 1812. Now he's hurt. Bad."

"Where is he?" asked Gran, looking around.

"I don't know. He took off. I hope he headed to town, but I'm not sure where he went. There was so much going on all at once. I should go after him."

"You do that." Gran glared at Luca. "It isn't over yet. I want you out of here. The Federals will be back. Next time it won't be some cockeyed cavalry fiasco. They'll come in force."

Luca heard a commotion. He turned to see wave after wave of blue-clad Union infantry advancing toward the Dimmock Line.

Chapter 29

Holding the Line

"Stay down and load; I'll shoot," Gran said. He gave Luca his Mississippi rifle, taking Luca's loaded gun.

Luca watched the wave grow closer until he could distinguish individual soldiers. A bullet whizzed by him. He fell to his knees and loaded Gran's gun.

Gran aimed and fired. He bent to take the Mississippi rifle from Luca. He eased himself up to where he could see above the earthwork, aimed, and fired. Then he tossed Luca the empty gun, and Luca loaded it while Gran aimed and fired again.

Bullets were coming fast. They hit the dirt of the earthwork and exploded with little showers of soil.

Luca peeked over the earthworks. Everywhere he looked, lines of Union soldiers were moving forward. "There are hundreds of them," he shouted, as he settled back behind the earthworks and bent to the task of reloading.

Above the din of shooting, Luca heard the rumble of wheels. Behind him, he saw a wagon lumber up. It contained a large field gun. "A 12-pounder!" Gran yelled as he bent to change guns. "A howitzer."

"Will it make a difference?"

"Some." Gran nodded toward the unloaded gun in Luca's hand. "Get that loaded."

Luca heard a tremendous roar as the earthwork eighty feet away exploded. Dirt flew everywhere, hitting the ground with a series of thuds. Screams followed the explosion. When the smoke and dust cleared, Luca saw that a whole section of the Dimmock Line had disappeared along with those who had defended it. He felt sick.

"The Union guns have found their range," Gran said as he bent to take a rifle from Luca.

The earth shook as Yankee cannon pounded the earthworks. Their roar overcame the sounds of the attackers. Luca's stomach heaved and his eyes burned from the gun smoke. His fingers flew as he skillfully loaded the guns Gran passed him. His grandfather's insistence on practice was paying off.

Luca finished loading a gun, but his grandfather didn't bend down to get it. Luca glanced up. His grandfather slumped against the earthwork. Blood oozed from a wound in his side.

"Gran!" Luca jumped to his feet. A bullet screamed by his ear, and he crouched instantly. He crawled over to his grandfather. "Gran?"

"Boy," Gran said, motioning with his hand, "there's a handkerchief in my pocket. Get it."

Luca reached into Gran's pocket and found the handkerchief. He knew immediately that it wasn't going to staunch the flow of blood. He took out his pocket knife, the one Gran had given him. "I'm going to cut away your shirt." With a strength Luca didn't know he had, he cut open Gran's shirt.

"God bless a blue-eyed black snake!" Gran winced from the pain and closed his eyes.

Luca ripped off his own shirt. It had been clean this morning, but now it was stained with sweat and dirt. He stuffed the handkerchief into the bloody wound. It turned instantly red. He folded his shirt into a bandage. "Lean forward a little," he said. Gran eased toward him and Luca secured the shirt, using the arms to tie it securely behind Gran's back. "That's the best I can do for now." Luca leaned back on his heels to study the bandage.

Above the roar of the cannon and turmoil around them, Luca became conscious of someone yelling. "Pull back! Pull back! We can't hold the line!" Luca glimpsed an officer in a Confederate uniform galloping along the line. All along the Dimmock Line, Luca saw the remnants of the Militia Reserves begin to withdraw.

"Gran, we've got to move back. Can you walk?"

"I'll try," Gran said, gritting his teeth. "But we've got to keep down."

Gran used the side of the earthwork to pull himself up almost to a standing position. His knees buckled once, but he managed to stand.

Luca was at his side. "Lean on me. Here, use your rifle for a walking stick."

There was no time for argument. Gran and Luca hobbled away from the earthworks. A shell exploded somewhere nearby, but they didn't even look to see where it had landed. Gran tottered and almost toppled as they made their way over the rough terrain that lay behind the earthwork.

Luca looked around for help. Men and boys scattered in every direction. Two men passed them, running as fast as if the devil himself were behind them. "Stop! Help us!" Luca called out, but they just kept running.

Luca propelled the old man away from the sounds of fighting. Gran was breathing heavily. Blood seeped through the makeshift bandage.

Luca looked around frantically. He had to find somewhere for them to hide, but where? There was a ravine off to their right. "This way," he said. He half pulled, half pushed his grandfather down the steep side of the ravine.

Gran gasped and almost fell. Luca realized they couldn't go much farther. Ahead were bushes overgrown with honeysuckle. "We're going to hide over there," he said.

Retreating soldiers
Drawing by W. L. Sheppard in *The Century*, 30 (June, 1885), p. 296

With one last effort, Gran stumbled forward. They reached the bushes and collapsed.

Luca sat for a moment catching his breath. Gran looked terrible. There was no color in his face and bright blood seeped through the makeshift bandage. "We've got to get behind those," Luca said, pointing to an especially thick clump of bushes. Dodging thick branches, Luca dragged Gran behind the screen of sweet-smelling honeysuckle.

Gran closed his eyes and Luca didn't know if he was unconscious or was just resting. Luca was breathing so hard he was sure that anyone who came close could hear him. Other members of the Militia Reserves came crashing through the ravine. A series of shots rang out. Luca guessed Union soldiers were close behind them.

Minutes passed. Luca's breathing grew easier. The ravine grew quiet except for the twittering of birds in the trees. Then in the stillness, Luca heard voices. Someone was coming.

Chapter 30

Hiding

Luca leaned forward to where he could peer through the honeysuckle. Cadaver Barnum and another man Luca didn't recognize came running down the side of the ravine from the direction of the Dimmock Line. He was just about to stand up and call for help when he saw Union soldiers appear at the top of the slope. "Halt, or we'll shoot!" one yelled.

Mr. Barnum and the other man stopped, dropped their weapons, and slowly turned around. The Yankee soldiers made their way into the ravine. "We surrender," said Mr. Barnum, putting his thin hands high in the air. The other man did the same.

"Sergeant, see to these two," said an officer. "Then I want you to take a couple of men and comb the area." The officer hurried back to the lip of the ravine to join a stream of bluecoats advancing toward Petersburg.

"Come on, you two," said the sergeant, a burly young man with a dark beard. Luca could see, even from a distance, that Mr. Barnum's hands were trembling. Luca had never liked Cadaver Barnum, but couldn't help feeling sorry for him now.

The sergeant didn't seem pleased with the task he had been assigned. "Stone, Ellis, Haines, come with me."

Gran stirred and groaned. Luca put his hand over his grandfather's mouth. Gran opened his eyes and then closed them again. In the commotion of taking the prisoners away, none of the Yankees heard the groan.

The sergeant and the men he had chosen disappeared up the side of the ravine with their prisoners. Luca looked about, wondering if there was a better place they could hide. He didn't see one, but when the Yankees came back, he planned to be ready.

Gran's Mississippi rifle lay at his side. Luca picked it up and loaded it, taking care to make as little noise as possible. He moved away from Gran until he was backed up against the side of the ravine. He angled the gun toward the spot where someone was most likely to discover them and rested the barrel on some branches.

Gran stirred and opened his eyes. "Boy," he called out. His voice was low and raspy. "My flask. In my pocket."

Luca went to his grandfather's side and gently patted the pockets of his coat. There was a silver flask in the breast pocket. Luca handed it to him.

Gran unscrewed the top. "Can you prop me up a little?"

Gran winced in pain as Luca helped raise his head and shoulders. Gran took a sip from the flask.

"Do you want some?" Gran asked.

"No sir." As he said the words, Luca realized his mouth was as dry as a burlap bag full of dust.

"Now take off the shirt, and pour the rest of the spirits over the wound."

Luca carefully untied the shirt and removed the blood-soaked handkerchief. He gagged when he saw the gaping hole in his grandfather's side.

"Do it carefully," Gran said. "Try to get as much of it as possible into the wound itself."

Struggling to keep his hand steady, Luca dribbled the whiskey onto the wound. Gran grimaced and didn't say anything until Luca had finished. "Now wrap it up again."

Luca retied his shirt around the wound and then returned to where he had set up the gun. Ten or fifteen minutes passed. Luca heard voices and looked out of the bushes. The Yankees were back. The same sergeant and the men who had taken charge of Mr. Barnum and the other man had returned to search the area.

"Jones, you take the left side of the ravine. Haines, you take the right. Ellis and I will follow the little stream, one on each side. And make it quick. We don't want to be here all day. We'll want to be with the regiment when they take Petersburg."

The men began searching the ravine. After a few minutes, Haines was the only one Luca could see. "Come out of there!" Haines said, taking the end of his gun and probing the bushes near the rim of the ravine. There was no response. He walked down the slope toward where Luca and Gran were hidden. Luca could see him clearly. Haines was young, probably only seventeen or eighteen with a pimply face and spiky blond hair sticking out from under his blue soldier's kepi.

"Come out of there!" Haines called again and again as he probed the bushes with his gun. No one answered. He was closer now. Luca could feel sweat roll down his back. His damp fingers rested on the trigger. In the distance he heard the courthouse clock toll the hour. It was twelve o'clock. The sound, so ordinary, so taken for granted in Petersburg, seemed out of place with a Yankee just feet away, pointing a gun in their direction.

Haines neared the bushes that sheltered them. He cautiously parted them with his rifle and saw Gran. "Come out of there, old man," he said.

"I can't," said Gran. "I don't think I can move."

"Come out or I'll shoot," said Haines, clearly rattled by the sight of the helpless old man.

"Don't you dare," said Luca. He tried to keep his voice firm and threatening, but he was sure that it sounded thin and childlike. "My gun will make... *maccheroni* of your chest."

Chapter 31

Standoff

Haines didn't say anything for a moment. He didn't seem to know what to do.

Luca leveled the rifle, pointing it directly at the soldier's chest. He hoped that Haines hadn't noticed he was shaking. "He's my grandfather," Luca blurted out. "He's an old man. If he's taken prisoner, he'll die."

"If you shoot me," Haines said, "the others will be on you in a minute."

"And you'll be dead," said Luca.

Haines seemed to think about this. Luca took advantage of the young man's uncertainty and said, "Just leave us. No one will know. Back away slowly and keep searching. Your sergeant doesn't want to find anyone. He's in a hurry to get to Petersburg. I heard him say so."

Haines took a step backward. "Stop pointing that gun at me. I'm not going to tell anyone. I've got a granddad myself. I didn't join up to fight little boys and old men." Haines was slowly backing away.

Luca lowered the rifle little by little. Haines turned and disappeared down the ravine. Luca rested the gun again on some bushes and lowered his head onto the barrel.

A few moments later, he returned to his watchful position. The day was hot, and he looked down at his undershirt and saw that it was stained with sweat and his grandfather's blood.

Fifteen or twenty minutes later, Haines finished. He met the others and they disappeared. In the distance, Luca heard rifle fire and the low muttering of artillery. It sounded like another battle was starting. He wondered if they were fighting in Petersburg itself. Gran opened his eyes, and they both listened to the distant crack of rifles. "I wonder what's going on," Luca said.

"They may be making a last stand in front of the city."

"Who's left to take a stand?"

"This morning the city council let the prisoners out of jail and armed the walking wounded from the hospitals. They sent them out to Blandford Church. Maybe they've fallen back to defend the city, and of course, there are two units of regulars out there somewhere."

"Is there any chance General Lee will send reinforcements?"

"I hope so," said Gran. He seemed in a daze, and even though he talked to Luca, Gran's attention was elsewhere.

The sun grew hotter in the afternoon and filtered through the trees. Luca developed a raging thirst. He knew there was a stream at the bottom of the ravine. He hadn't seen it, but the soldiers had mentioned it.

"Gran, what if I went down to that stream and filled your flask with water? I haven't seen any bluecoats for a while."

"I'd surely like a drink, but if the Union army are driven back, they'll come this way. It's too risky just now."

Gran fell into a fitful doze. Luca kept watching for Yankees. Occasionally, he saw soldiers on the distant ridge. He tried not to think about going for a drink of water. He wondered what would happen to them if the Yankees had taken Petersburg. What was the point of hiding if they were to become prisoners anyway? Maybe he'd been wrong to bring Gran here.

Luca was overwhelmed with the thought that he'd done nothing right. His mother was alone and unprotected in Petersburg. Gran had taught him to shoot in case the Yankees took the city. Now the Yankees were headed for Petersburg, and his mother was undefended. His grandfather had repeatedly told him to think, and all Luca thought about today was taking part in the defense of the city. He hadn't thought about his mother at all. And he felt awful about Jim. Why hadn't they included Jim in their target practice? He had obviously never fired that old, rusty gun. His terrible accident could have been avoided, if only Luca had thought about his friend instead of always thinking about himself. If all this wasn't bad enough, he should have told Gran about Eli. Today's disaster might have been prevented.

Time passed slowly. The shadows lengthened, and Luca heard the courthouse clock strike four. It had been a long time since he and Gran had heard the sounds of battle. Now and then Luca heard rifle fire, but it had been at least an hour or more since he'd seen any soldiers. He put down the gun and picked up Gran's flask. "Gran," he said. His grandfather opened his eyes. "I'm going for water. I'll be right back."

"Be careful."

Luca headed toward the stream. He moved through the woods cautiously, stopping every little while to listen. He heard water gurgling before he saw it. The stream was full and fast-moving from the recent rains. His thirst drove him forward. When he reached the stream, he knelt on the mossy bank and put his whole face into the rushing water. Delicious coolness flooded over him. He drank deeply. He had never drunk anything half so good. He pulled his face from the water. That bothersome lock of hair that was always falling onto his forehead dripped water into his eyes. He brushed it away and looked around.

Twenty feet from where he had drunk was a body. Luca recoiled in horror.

Chapter 32

The Dead Man

Luca wanted to run. Instead, he forced himself to walk over to the still figure. The man lay face down. He wasn't wearing a uniform. He must be someone from town. He didn't move. Luca knew he should touch him, see if he was still alive, but he couldn't. He knew the man was dead. His skin was gray, almost the color of ashes, and there were red-brown bloodstains on his shirt and jacket.

The sight brought Gran to mind. Was Gran dying? He looked down at the flask that he still held in his hand. He moved away from the dead man, knelt, and washed it out. He filled it with water and turned back toward where he had left his grandfather.

"Gran," Luca said when he returned, "see if you can drink a little of this." He held the flask to Gran's lips and the old man drank a few mouthfuls. The water seemed to revive him, and he drank some more.

"There's a dead man face down in the stream," said Luca.

"Are you sure he's dead?"

"He's dead for sure. He looks pretty bad."

"Do you know who it is?"

"It's somebody from town. I don't recognize him. What should we do?"

"There's nothing we can do now. When whatever is going on is over, they will send out details to collect the dead and wounded."

"Who are *they?*"

"If we've driven the Yankees back, it'll be a detail from the Militia Reserves. In that case, we'll be all set. If it's a detail of bluecoats, I want you to skedaddle. When I'm sure you're safely away, I'll call for help."

It was clear to Luca that Gran had been thinking this over. "I don't want to leave you, Gran."

"You'll have to if the Federals have won. Staying with me would make as much sense as a chicken walking up to a housewife and telling her to wring its neck. Right now we'll just have to wait and see."

Luca wanted to talk more about this, but his grandfather spoke with such tiredness and such finality that Luca kept silent. He heard the distant clatter of horses' hooves and the creak of wagons. Then it grew quiet. He closed his eyes. The clock on the courthouse struck five and then six and seven. He awoke with a start when he heard voices in the distance. He sat up abruptly. He nudged Gran, who didn't open his eyes.

Luca looked out of the bushes as he had so many times that day. He saw no one. He wondered if he should call out. Maybe he had already waited too long to get help for Gran. Who had won today? Did it really matter who had won if Gran was dead?

The sun sank below the trees at the top of the ravine and disappeared. As dusk gathered, Luca knew he had to do something. But he didn't know what.

Where were the soldiers the victors sent out for the dead and wounded? Why hadn't they come for them?

In the waning light, Luca saw two people on the rim of the ridge; one was tall and dark, and the other was a woman. He looked hard at them, not believing what he was seeing. "Madre," he said out loud. He stood and crashed out of the bushes. "Madre!" he called out. "Madre, we're over here!"

Luca ran toward the two figures. Mrs. Streetman hurried toward her son. Luca fell into her arms.

"Luca, Luca!" Madre cried as her arms encircled him. Tears ran down her face. She began speaking rapidly in Italian. She was so worried about him. She was so glad he was safe. He had been thoughtless to go off with the others. He was too young...

"Gran's hurt," Luca said, interrupting her in midsentence. "We've got to help him."

"Where is he?" a voice said.

Luca looked up. A man stood just behind Madre. It was Eli. Luca was taken aback. What was Eli, of all people, doing here?

"Where is he?" Eli asked again.

"Back there. I'll take you," Luca said. "I think he's unconscious. He needs a doctor."

Eli seemed to sum up the situation in an instant. "I'll take him to the hospital," he said. He stooped and picked up the unconscious Gran as easily and as gently as if he were a child. "There's no time to lose. I'm going to cut through the woods. You best take the boy home on the road."

"Thank you, Eli," said Madre. "Thank you for coming with me."

"Glad to do it, ma'am," said Eli as he headed off with Gran.

Luca picked up Gran's Mississippi rifle. He and Madre climbed out of the ravine to the road. They walked arm in arm toward town. Madre refused to let go of him, even for a second.

"Promise me you'll never do anything like this again," said Madre.

"That's an easy promise to make. Today was pretty awful. I have no idea how you found us, how you were able to find us. What happened to the Yankees?"

"I don't know where to begin. It looked like the city was doomed until reinforcement arrived. They drove back the Union army this afternoon. I didn't realize you'd gone with the others until Emmy found me at the hospital. The remnant of the Militia Reserves had long since returned, and you weren't with them. Then townspeople began bringing in the dead and the wounded, and you weren't among them." His mother began to cry.

"I'm sorry, Madre."

Madre wiped her tears and continued, "I asked anyone and everyone who had been with the Militia Reserves if they'd seen you. The Leighton boy told me that he saw you retreating with your grandfather. He thought you were headed for the ravine. I wanted to go and look for you, but there was no one I could call on for help. Then, I thought of Eli. I went to Miss Maizie's and asked him if he'd come with me. We were going to search the ravine before dark. Thank God, you saw us. We never could have found you."

"Why hasn't the Milita Reserves sent out search parties?"

"They have. But they've been overwhelmed. There are a lot of wounded and dead on both sides."

It was dark when they reached the house on High Street. "Sit down," Madre said. "You must be starved. I'll get you something to eat. It won't take me a moment."

Luca sat at the kitchen table. While Madre went to the pantry, he put his head down on the table. He closed his eyes and slept.

"Bang, bang, bang." Luca struggled up from the depth of sleep. Someone was at the door.

Chapter 33

Looking for Jim

Luca rubbed his eyes. Madre went to the door and opened it. Luca stood and walked to the hallway.

Emmy and Jim's mother stood in the doorway. "Come in," Madre said. Luca was surprised to see Mrs. Prentice with Emmy. Jim's mother looked pale and drawn, but she didn't appear to be the same invalid that Luca had seen sitting on the front porch earlier that day.

Emmy and Mrs. Prentice came in. "Jim still hasn't shown up. We heard that you'd found Luca," said Emmy. "Could we talk to him?"

"Certainly," said Madre. She turned to see Luca standing behind her. "Let's go into the kitchen. Luca hasn't had anything to eat yet. There's plenty for everybody."

"Thank you, but we've eaten," said Mrs. Prentice. "We're hoping Luca can tell us something about Jim."

Madre put the teakettle on the stove. She poured Luca and Emmy glasses of milk and put a platter of ham biscuits and a plate of sugar cookies on the table.

"Have you checked the hospitals?" asked Luca. "His gun exploded the first time he tried to fire it. The last time I saw him he was headed for town."

Tears rose to Emmy's eyes and she sniffled as she struggled for self-control, but she didn't cry. "We've been to all the hospitals. No one's seen him. Uncle Pete and I searched around Battery 27 until it got dark," she said.

"I thought he was going for help. I wanted to follow him, but the next thing I knew the Yankees were on us," said Luca.

"We're not blaming you," said Mrs. Prentice. "We thought you might have some idea of where he might be."

An image of the man Luca had seen dead by the creek flashed into his mind. He hadn't thought Jim was badly hurt, but maybe he'd been worse off than Luca realized.

"Jim told me that one day you and he went to a hideout in the woods," said Emmy. "Could he have gone there?"

"More than likely he's in the ravine where Gran and I hid from the Yankees," said Luca. "I can't imagine why he'd go to the hideout. It doesn't make sense."

"You know Jim," said Emmy. "What doesn't make sense to anyone else might make perfect sense to him. Besides, there's no place else left for us to look until morning."

"Will you take us there?" asked Mrs. Prentice. "We're grasping at straws now."

The teakettle started to boil, and Madre poured Mrs. Prentice a cup of peppermint tea. Luca looked for a moment at his mother. After what she had gone through this day, he didn't want her to worry anymore.

"Mrs. Prentice," said Madre, "I know how worried you are, but why don't you stay here with me? You're looking awfully tired. Luca can show Emmy the place."

"We have to find Jim! I'm afraid something awful has happened to him," Mrs. Prentice said, her voice shaking. "Emmy can go with Luca if you think that is best."

"Eat something now," Madre said to Luca. "I'll light the lantern. Tell me exactly where you're going."

Luca told Madre about the big holly tree not far from the Adams farm. Then he ate several ham biscuits and drank the milk. He stood and stuffed three cookies into his pocket.

"Come on, Emmy," he said.

Luca and Emmy went out into the night. Everything was quiet. Neither of them felt like talking. "It's so quiet, it's eerie," said Luca. "It's almost as if the whole town is resting up after the battle."

They walked until they came to the place on the road where the trail led off into the woods. "I want you to stay here," said Luca. "There's a chance Jim could be in the hideout, and just as big a chance that somebody else could be there."

"I've come this far. I want to go with you."

"I want you to come with me too. But if I don't come back, even with the directions I gave Madre, no one could find this spot. Will you stay here, and if I'm not back in twenty minutes, go for help?"

"All right."

Luca felt bad leaving Emmy alone in the dark. "I'll be back as soon as I can."

Luca started down the path. In the dim light of the lantern, everything looked different. The overhanging vines and trees seemed threatening, and the lantern cast weird shadows as he made his way deeper into the woods.

When he reached the fallen oak, he knew he had found the right place. "Jim," he called out softly, "Jim, are you there? It's Luca."

"Go away," came the muffled reply. "Just leave me alone."

Chapter 34

Gran

Luca climbed on top of the fallen tree and a moment later was in the little clearing. He went to where the boys had dug the earthwork and the cave. He held his lantern over the cave entrance. He couldn't see anything in the dim light. He held his breath and went into the opening. Jim lay near the back wall, curled up like an unborn baby. "What's the matter, Jim? Why didn't you go to the hospital?"

"I couldn't." Jim struggled to sit up in the small space, and Luca noticed that his right eye was swollen shut. He looked awful.

"And why not? You need to be treated."

"I soiled myself." Jim began to sob. "I'm ashamed."

"You needn't be. Grown men did the same today and worse. The river's over there. You can wash a little and we'll go back."

"I've washed already. But I can't go back."

"No one ever has to know. No one, unless you tell them. Emmy is waiting at the road. I didn't like leaving her alone. But I didn't know what or whom I'd find here. Your mother's at my house."

"My mother?"

"Yes, she wanted to come with us, but Madre convinced her to wait there. She looks worn out. Come on, let's go. If we're not back soon, Emmy will have half the town out here."

Jim didn't resist. Luca helped him out of the cave, and they made their way back to the road. As they came out of the thick woods, Luca called out, "Emmy! Emmy! I've got him!"

A moment later, her dark shape joined them in the circle of light cast by the lantern. "Jim," she said, her voice full of relief, "I'm so glad we've found you. Are you all right?"

Luca held the lantern up a little so she could see Jim's face. Emmy gasped. "Oh, Jim! I'm sorry. It must hurt awfully."

"I'm glad you found me," Jim said, his voice thick with emotion.

"When we reach town, I'm taking Jim directly to the Confederate States Hospital," Luca said to Emmy. "Can you get your mother and bring her there?"

"Of course, silly," said Emmy, some of her old spirit returning.

Later when Luca got home, Madre was waiting for him. "I know it's been a difficult day," she said, "and I've been debating whether to tell you something now or wait until tomorrow. I decided I'd tell you now."

"It isn't Gran, is it?"

"No, your Aunt Lucy stopped here on her way home from the hospital. She said your grandfather is holding his own." She paused for a moment. "One of the boys your age was killed in the battle. Shot through the heart. His name was Freddie Purdy."

Luca took a deep breath and shook his head in disbelief. He had not liked Freddie Purdy, but he had never wished him dead.

"I'm going to bed. I'm exhausted," said Luca. He gave Madre a long hug before heading toward the stairs.

In the hallway, Luca spotted his box of toy soldiers on the stand where he had left them last week. He picked up the box and carried it to his room. He had a small chest in which he kept treasures that he had outgrown. He put the soldiers into the chest next to *The Big Book of Favorite Fairytales*.

As worn out as he felt, Luca couldn't sleep that night. He had dozed in the thicket and then fallen asleep at the table. Those two brief episodes now made sleep impossible. His brain reeled with horrible images of the battle, and he felt terrible about Jim.

Luca had failed his friend, and it wasn't only that he hadn't thought to include Jim in target practices. In his heart Luca knew he had always been disloyal to Jim, wanting to join Jake and his group. Now that disloyalty haunted him.

And Eli, why hadn't Luca shared his suspicions with Gran? If only Luca and Jim had taken the map and the drawings from the Trapezium House, they could have proven that Eli was part of a spy ring. Perhaps the disaster at Battery 27 could have been avoided. If Eli was working for the Union army, why had he helped Madre tonight? Luca had thought that Eli was an enemy, but now he was no longer sure.

The sky was growing light when Luca finally fell into a troubled sleep. When he woke, it was already afternoon. He found his mother sitting in the kitchen.

"Have you heard how Jim and Gran are doing?" he asked.

"Emmy came here this morning. She said they've sent Jim home. He's burned, but he's a very lucky boy. Apparently, he didn't aim the gun when he fired it. If he'd done it properly, he probably would have lost an eye or been killed. It seems he held it at arm's length and hadn't loaded it correctly. His hands are burned and one side of his face, but it could be much worse."

"And how's Gran?"

"He's holding his own."

"I want to see Gran as soon as I've washed and eaten. I need to talk with him." He had made up his mind to tell Gran everything.

"I'll go with you. I've been neglecting my hospital work. I'm sure they could use my help."

An hour later, Luca found Gran in the first big open ward of the hospital. It wasn't a good place to talk.

"Boy," Gran said when he approached the bed.

"How are you, Gran?"

"I feel like I'm a plucked chicken the way that surgeon picked over my wound. He seemed surprised that there was so little infection. He wanted to cut out the bullet. I said no. I told him I'd been abused enough for now."

"There's some things I have to tell you." Luca looked around, wondering if this was the appropriate time and place.

"I have something to give you." Gran took his watch from the rough, wooden box that served for a stand beside the bed. "Your grandmother gave this to me, Luca. And I want you to have it."

Luca was stunned. His grandfather hadn't called him "boy." And he hadn't called him "Luke," either.

Instead, he had called him by his name. And his grand-father wanted to give him his watch. Did that mean he was dying? "I can't take your watch," Luca said, unsure how to respond. "Shouldn't my father have it?"

"He has a fine watch. I know. I bought it for him. For years I've hung on to this one." He fingered the fine gold watch. "Mrs. S. was your grandmother's best friend. When I asked Mrs. S. to marry me, I told her that I'd always love your grandmother, and Mrs. S. took me on anyway. And over the years Mrs. S. and I have done fine. Then you and your mother came to town. Of course Mrs. S. and my girls always knew about my first family. But it's one thing for a mother cat to have her kittens in the barn, and yet another for her to bring them into the house. It's been hard on Mrs. S. and your aunts. You have your grandmother's smile and you favor her right much." He held the watch out to Luca.

"I can't take it, Gran. You'll need it."

"Boy," said Gran in that tone of voice that allowed no contradiction. Luca reached out and took it.

"Thank you, Gran."

"We'll talk tomorrow; I'm tired now. The doctor is letting Mrs. S. take me home this evening."

Luca turned to go. He held his grandfather's watch tightly in his hand. His eyes filled with tears and his thoughts flew. Did this mean his grandfather wouldn't need his watch anymore? Was the doctor sending him home to die?

Chapter 35

Fine Friend

Luca saw Dr. Jenkins near the main door of the hospital. He wore a leather apron, and he was washing his hands in a basin. The doctor seemed to have aged in the short time since Luca had visited the hospital with Madre. The doctor's eyes were red-rimmed and his clothes were rumpled.

"Pardon me, sir, but can you tell me how Mr. Streetman is doing?" Luca asked.

The doctor looked up. "It could go either way," he said in a flat, tired voice. "The old man is so stubborn he wouldn't let me operate. And I didn't have the time or the energy to argue with him. It's out of my hands." Luca's face must have fallen because the doctor's tone softened. "But if I were a betting man, I'd bet that old man is too ornery to die, just yet."

Luca felt relief spill over him as if someone had doused him with a bucket of cold water on a hot day. So much had happened in such a short time, he was finding it difficult to sort it all out. If Gran was going to be okay, maybe he would help Luca understand the mysterious goings on at Miss Maizie's. Perhaps Gran would know what mischief Eli was up to.

Luca went from the hospital to Jim's house. "How's Jim?" he asked when Mrs. Prentice answered the door.

"He's awake, and I know he'd love to see you. Emmy's helping the women at church make bandages. Thank you for finding Jim," Mrs. Prentice said, giving Luca a warm, sincere smile.

"Emmy helped."

"She's a good girl. I've always known that, but yesterday she was my strength."

"It looks like you're feeling better yourself," said Luca, noticing that Mrs. Prentice was still thin and pale, but no longer had the deadly pallor of a sick person.

"After Jim and Emmy's father died, I thought my life was over. Yesterday when Jim disappeared, I realized that I'd let my grief overshadow my blessings. Things will be different now," she said, as she led Luca upstairs to a small room.

Luca had never been in Jim's room, but it was exactly how he had imagined it. Books were everywhere. A bookcase was crammed full. Piles of books littered the floor, the dresser, and the room's only chair. Jim lay in bed, propped up with pillows. His face, hands, and arms were swathed in bandages.

"You look like a mummy," said Luca.

"Thanks," said Jim. "I feel like burnt toast."

"If there's nothing you need, Jim, I'll leave you two to talk," said Mrs. Prentice, heading back down the stairs.

When she was out of earshot, Jim said, "My mother's been up and down the stairs four times this morning already. And just yesterday, she could hardly make it up one flight to her own room. My accident has had at least one good effect."

"I'm glad. I need to talk to you." Luca felt his face getting red. "I feel it's my *colpa*...er, I mean...fault you're in this bed."

Jim laughed. He must have thought Luca's Italian gaffe was intentional.

Luca continued, "It never occurred to me that you hadn't practiced with your gun. I was so busy learning to shoot with my grandfather that I forgot all about you. Fine friend I am."

"It was an oversight. I should have known better. I should have taken better care of my father's gun. What bothers me is that now everyone will know about my...accident."

"I thought you didn't care what people thought."

"Well, I have a reputation...of sorts...to maintain."

"Were you scared?"

"Not really, I was just thinking of the trajectory of the bullets whizzing by and not really paying attention to what I was doing. Then once the gun exploded, I had no control over my bowels. So now, I'll not only be a brain, but a baby."

Only Jim would use a word like bowels, thought Luca. "You told me that you didn't mind being a brain," said Luca. "And no one has to know about the other."

"I know."

"And I know I should have been a better friend to you. I'm sure you heard about Freddie and Eddie tying me up. Since I didn't go on and on about it, and Gran or Madre didn't make a fuss, the incident died right there. I won't tell anybody about your accident...and I'm sure it's not something you want to talk about."

"From this moment on, I'll never mention it again. Tell me about what happened yesterday during the battle," said Jim, changing the subject.

Luca told Jim about what had happened at Battery 27, hiding in the ravine, and Eli coming to their rescue. "I'm so confused now about Eli and that whole business, I just can't make any sense of it."

"Did it occur to you that helping your grandfather has convinced everyone of Eli's loyalty?"

"You mean that Eli's playing all the angles?"

"Of course. Wouldn't you, if you were a slave?"

"Well, Eli was only one part of the spy ring. It's all over town that Carter Wiley is missing and he wasn't at Battery 27."

"Do you think he was the man in the Trapezium House?"

"It could be. Wiley has a bum leg and whoever was in the house didn't run after us."

"The whole thing's beyond me. I feel...responsible. If only I'd told Gran about Eli. If only I'd taken the map..."

When Luca left Jim's house later that afternoon, he vowed that things would be different from now on. He'd try hard to be a good friend to Jim.

As he walked toward the center of town, he saw signs of mourning everywhere. Men in the street wore black armbands, and when he passed St. Paul's Episcopal Church, there was a funeral going on inside. He saw Jake Leighton, dressed in his best suit, standing out in front with several boys.

"It's so crowded we can't even get in the door."

"Whose funeral is it?" asked Luca.

"The druggist, Mr. Crowder. They found him in the ravine."

Luca didn't know the man. He had seen him in the drugstore, and he knew that he had a big family, six or seven children. He wondered if Crowder was the same man he had seen in the creek. "I'm sorry for his family."

"There's a lot of sorry families in Petersburg today. Sixty percent of the Militia Reserves is either dead, wounded, or taken prisoner. I heard that the bluebellies sent 3,500 infantry and 1,400 cavalry at us."

"There sure were a lot of them."

"Some townspeople are comparing our stand at Battery 27 to the stand of the three hundred Spartans at the Battle of Thermopylae."

"What are you talking about?" Luca had heard of the famous battle between the Greeks and Persians in the Persian Wars, but he was sure Jake never had before today.

"That old windbag from the library is down at the courthouse. He's telling everyone about the Spartans who died defending a pass to save Greece two thousand years ago. I guess they're making the comparison because we were stationed where the Union army tried to break through the Dimmock Line on Jerusalem Plank Road. And by holding out as long as we did, we saved the day. Did you know your grandfather has been bragging about you?"

"No," said Luca, surprised at this information.

"He's telling everyone who will listen that you faced down a Yankee and told him you'd make macaroni of his chest if he didn't back off."

"It was a dumb thing to say." Luca smiled. "And I said it in Italian."

"Everybody thinks you're a hero," said Jake, a bit enviously.

Luca was startled. He hadn't been a hero. When the Yankee, Haines, had found them, he had never been more frightened in his life. He hadn't done anything. He'd only reacted, desperately trying to save his grandfather from certain death in a Union prison. He looked at Jake to make sure that he was serious, and Luca became aware of the fact that Ben wasn't with Jake. "Where's Ben?" Luca asked, almost afraid of what the answer would be.

"Both Ben and his father have been taken prisoner."

"I'm sorry. Are you going to Freddie's funeral on Sunday?"

"All the guys are going." Just then the doors of the church opened, and people poured into the street like ants from a disturbed anthill.

"See you Sunday," said Luca. He hurried off to avoid the crush of people. On the way home, he thought over what Jake had said about Thermopylae. He didn't like the idea of people making the militia stand at Battery 27 into something heroic. It had been more horrible than heroic.

Chapter 36

Enemies in our Midst

Luca went to his grandfather's house the following day. Mrs. S. greeted him at the door. "Come in, come in," she said, all aflutter. "Mr. S. is expecting you." She paused for a moment. "Thank you, Luke, I mean, Luc...a, thank you for giving Mr. S. back to us. It was silly, I know, but when you and your mother came to town, I was afraid you'd take him from us. You favor your grandmother so much, I was jealous. I'm sorry. It was a mistake."

Luca didn't know what to say. It did sound silly to him, but it explained why she and his aunts had been cool. Before he could respond, she took his hand and led him into his grandfather's study. The desk had been pushed aside to make room for a bed. Gran was propped up on several pillows, sipping a glass of water and looking much better.

"Thank you, Mrs. S.," Gran said. "We'll be fine." He dismissed her with a wave of his hand.

"How are you feeling?" Luca asked.

"These women don't leave a man alone. Why, every time I make a move, one of them comes in to see if

I want anything. They're like a swarm of bees around a honey pot."

Luca now knew his grandfather well enough to know that even though he complained, he was enjoying the attention of his wife and daughters. "So, you're feeling a bit better," Luca ventured.

"Boy, what did you want to see me about?"

Luca told his grandfather about all the strange things that have been happening and what made him think Eli was a spy.

Gran chuckled. "Ooh, that hurt," he said, lightly touching the bandages on his side.

Luca was upset. "Gran, this is not a joke. I'm serious. If I had told you this before, maybe the Militia Reserves wouldn't have borne the brunt of the Union attack."

"I didn't mean that it was a joke. It's just that you have supplied pieces of a puzzle that I've been trying to figure out."

"What should we do about Eli? I'm convinced he's a spy. For weeks I thought he was our enemy, but after the other night, I'm confused."

"Things get complicated," Gran said. "He probably saved my life. He didn't have to go with your mother."

"You don't know Madre very well," Luca said with a smile.

"I plan to correct that oversight as soon as the sawbones lets me out of this blasted bed, but back to Eli. You've probably heard that Carter Wiley has disappeared. He didn't show up at Battery 27, even though he volunteered for the Militia Reserves. I was surprised that he showed up on May 5. Before the war, he was a

Union sympathizer, violently opposed to secession. Everyone is pretty sure that he went over to the Yankees the night before the attack. Now I know that he brought them a map and the plans for Pate's gun."

"But what about Eli?"

"A cynic could say that Eli was helping your mother only to mislead everyone. That may be the case, but I think not. I've known Eli since he was no taller than a pickle-barrel at McIlwaine's store. He knows I've been a good friend to Miss Maizie through the years. And whatever he may be up to, he's loyal to Miss Maizie. What you've got to understand is that as long as there are slaves in the city, we are harboring enemies in our midst."

"But what if Eli gives more information to the Yankees?"

"He's not likely to. Carter Wiley is Miss Maizie's only living relative, her cousin's grandson. He probably threatened Eli, saying he would have Miss Maizie declared insane unless Eli got information for him."

"So, Eli was helping him in order to protect Miss Maizie, and it was Carter Wiley who was in the Trapezium House." Luca's head was spinning. "But, Gran," he said, trying to sort through everything that had happened, "I'm still confused about all this business with Eli. What about the strange things going on at Miss Maizie's?"

"There have been strange things going on there for years. Ever since..."

"Ever since what, Gran?"

"I've never told this to anyone. Miss Maizie's husband was a friend of mine. We went to grammar school together. He's been dead for years. Before he died, he told me what had happened and asked me to keep my eye on her. I'll tell you this, but I don't want you to tell anyone."

"Not even Jim?"

"Well, I guess it's all right if you tell Jim. But no one else. And swear him to secrecy. It's not a pretty story. Miss Maizie was born in the West Indies where her father grew sugar cane. Her parents died in a yellow fever epidemic, and she was brought to Petersburg to be looked after by her uncle, that fellow O'Hara I told you about. The man who owned the Trapezium House, the house everyone in town thinks is cursed. As a small child, Maizie lived in the Trapezium House. O'Hara hired a series of nurses and governesses, none of whom stayed very long. Finally, Maizie's widowed aunt, her mother's sister, came to town to take care of her. The aunt refused to live in the Trapezium House, and O'Hara provided her with a house in town where she raised Miss Maizie and her own daughter." Gran paused for a moment.

"So, Miss Maizie started acting strange after living in the Trapezium House?" Luca asked.

"There's more to it than that. Miss Maizie grew up and married. A year or two later, she lost a baby. It only lived a couple of days, and she almost died of childbirth fever. When she was out of her head, her cousin Jane pretended that the doll Pat was Miss Maizie's baby. Why she did this is unclear. The cousin's been dead now for twenty years. In any case, when Miss Maizie found out her baby was dead, and she had been cradling Pat instead, she went out of her head. Over the years, she's gotten better, and sometimes she's quite sane."

"I picked up Pat and she is awfully heavy. So I naturally thought something was hidden inside. It made me wonder if Miss Maizie was somehow involved in a spy ring."

Gran shook his head. "I suspect Miss Maizie's cousin Jane put something heavy inside of Pat to make the doll seem more like a real baby. I can't imagine anything important is hidden inside."

"But what about the pins and all the packages going to and from the house?"

"Miss Maizie has her quirks and one of them is that she anonymously helps poor folk in town through hard times with food, clothes, and money. And whenever one of them has a baby she outfits it, sewing the baby clothes herself. I suspect that any pins are from her sewing, and any packages are food and clothes that Eli collects to distribute for her."

"Why doesn't Miss Maizie go outside?"

"She does go out occasionally," Gran said, "but she's old and she knows people think her odd. So she keeps pretty much to herself."

"What about Eli? If Miss Maizie's so kindhearted why hasn't she freed him?"

"When she changed her will recently, she made Eli her heir. He will have his freedom no matter how the war ends."

"Does Eli know what's in the will?"

"I suspect not," said Gran. "I only know because at the time she changed her will, she asked me to witness it."

"What about Sara, that awful woman who works for Miss Maizie?"

"I know that it's said around town that Sara has a hold on Miss Maizie. I suspect Sara is spreading those stories herself. She's laying the groundwork to take over Boadicea's business when the old woman dies. Sara has been doing everything possible to convince the whole town that she has special powers. She probably stuck pins in Pat and started those stories about Miss Maizie and her neighbor."

"Why do you suppose Miss Maizie keeps Sara on? Doesn't she know Sara's spreading stories about her?"

"Probably not. Keep in mind that Boadicea was O'Hara's servant for years and years. Miss Maizie's ties to Sara's family go way back."

Gran moved uneasily as if he were in pain. "All this palaver is wearing me down. I feel like I wrestled a mule and lost. But let's finish this business once and for all. Is there anything else?"

"What about the pig's head and the catfish?"

"The pig's head most probably came from Jordan. Remember, Jordan worked for Wiley as a body servant and errand boy. Jordan was undoubtedly picking up the information Eli left in the woodpile and taking it to Wiley. He may have thought the pouch had something to do with voodoo. The pig's head was supposed to scare off you and Jim."

"Why did Jordan turn pale when I went to show the pig's head to him?"

"He probably thought that the thing was evil. And he was convinced of it when it disappeared. He's pretty superstitious, and with Sara his aunt and Boadicea his grandmother he has reason to be. Probably a dog or a coon carried off the pig's head. As for the catfish, I can't imagine why Sara wanted it. She may like to eat catfish. Some folks do. Either that, or she was making a potion with it. Boadicea and Sara are always dabbling in some secret remedy or spell. They sell cures for everything, except death, and I expect they're working on that."

"What do you suppose Eli was doing with Miss Maizie in the garden?"

"That's easy. Miss Maizie's cat, Queen of Sheba, died. She was nearly twenty years old and she'd been poorly for months. Eli was probably just burying her."

"I can understand why Eli was helping Wiley. But Eli was still spying."

"Stop worrying about all this," said Gran. "Eli may have saved my life. What do you want me to do? Accuse him of spying? Besides, we have no proof. I hate this war."

"But you fought at Battery 27."

"I didn't have any choice. All these women folk are my responsibility." Gran waved his hand in the direction of the parlor. "Don't think I enjoyed it. Hell, full of fire and fiends, and meeting the devil himself, could be no worse than being in battle."

"But you fought in the Mexican War."

"Yes, and it was so terrible I don't even like to talk about it. I thought I was smart in getting your father out of war's way by steering him into diplomatic service. When I saw you at Battery 27 with the other boys, I felt like I had saved the lion at the cost of the cub. I could have bellied up right on the spot."

Luca was used to Gran's roundabout way of getting to the point, but it took him a minute to understand what his grandfather meant.

Gran turned a little in the bed and grimaced. "I've heard you out," he said. "Now there are two things I want you to do for me. Have you still got my gun?"

Chapter 37

Slaves Aren't Allowed

That afternoon, Luca went to Miss Maizie's house, carrying a basket and his grandfather's Mississippi rifle. The recently polished brass on the gun glinted in the sunlight as he stood at the garden gate and called out to Eli who was weeding the flowers. "May I speak with you a moment?" Luca asked, conscious suddenly that he had never exchanged more than a few words with the big man.

Eli stood and walked to the garden gate. "What is it?" Eli's face was stony, but he opened the gate and came to where Luca stood.

Luca put the basket down and extended the rifle to Eli. "Gran wants you to have this."

Eli just stood there. "Surely Mr. Streetman knows slaves aren't allowed to carry guns."

"Gran told me to say thank you and to say that those Yankees aren't through with Petersburg yet. He said you might need the rifle to look after Miss Maizie." Luca offered the rifle again to Eli.

Eli still didn't take the gun. His face revealed nothing, and he spoke with his usual sober dignity. "Your grandfather may think that it's all right for me to have a gun, but I'm not sure the rest of Petersburg would agree."

Luca pushed the hair off his forehead with his free hand. "Gran told me to tell you that if anyone had any problems with you having his rifle, to tell them to see him."

"People might react first and ask questions later," Eli said.

"Gran said you'd know better than to wave a red flag in front of a bull."

"I don't know how to shoot."

"Gran says as soon as he can get out of bed, he'll show you. He's a pretty good teacher," Luca said, pausing for a moment before he continued, "if you don't mind getting yelled at."

The slight hint of a smile softened Eli's face. He reached out and took the gun. "I want to say thank you, too," Luca said.

"I was glad to help, Master Luca. Tell your grandfather, I'll not betray his trust."

"Gran said he'd trust you with his life." Luca smiled his crooked smile.

"Please tell your mama I've got cucumber plants to give her. I'll leave them tomorrow in the shade of the dogwood in your garden."

"I'll tell her. I've also got a gift from Gran for Miss Maizie."

"I'll tell Miss Maizie. First, I better put the gun out of sight."

Eli left and returned a few moments later and led Luca into the sitting room where Miss Maizie was knitting.

"Good afternoon, Luca. You caught me at work," she said. "Eli tells me that you and your grandfather had quite an adventure. I want to hear all about it."

"Yes, ma'am. I'll be glad to tell you about the battle. But first I have something for you from Gran."

"For me?" Miss Maizie was as excited as a child.

"Inside the basket," said Luca, handing it to her.

Luca had put a red-checkered kitchen towel over the top of the basket to protect the contents from the sun, and now Miss Maizie carefully removed the towel. "Oh!" she said with obvious delight. "She's beautiful!" She reached into the basket and took out a sleepy, six-week-old kitten. The kitten was an unusual pinky-white color.

"Gran said to tell you that ever since Queen of Sheba died, he's been looking for just the right kitten for you," said Luca, struggling to remember everything Gran had told him to say. "When he found this one, he knew it would suit you, but he had to wait until she was weaned."

"She looks like peaches and cream. I'll call her Peaches." Miss Maizie put the kitten on the rug. Peaches looked about for a moment and then headed toward Miss Maizie's knitting basket where she swatted at the ball of blue yarn.

Miss Maizie laughed. "She's darling. Thank your grandfather for me."

"Gran told me to thank you for letting Eli go with my mother to search for us."

"Eli goes wherever's necessary and does what needs to be done. He always has. That's the way we've arranged things."

Peaches hooked her tiny claws into the ball of yarn. It rolled. The startled kitten hung on for dear life. Luca and Miss Maizie laughed.

At that moment Sara arrived with a pot of tea and a plate of cookies. She scowled at the kitten.

"I want to hear about how you and your grandfather escaped the Federals." Miss Maizie poured Luca a cup of tea and then poured cream into a saucer for the kitten.

Chapter 38

Anybody's Hero

The day of Freddie's funeral was clear and bright. Roses were in bloom, and to Luca it seemed wrong somehow that it was such a pretty June day. He and his mother arrived early at Washington Street Methodist Church for the service. The church soon filled with mourners.

Freddie's family came in last. His mother was rigid as she walked to the front of the church in a shabby, black dress. She carried a baby in her arms, and a child of perhaps three or four walked at her side. Freddie's father wore a battered-looking top hat and suit that had grown shiny with wear. A boy about eight years old in a suit too large for him walked by his father's side.

When the service began, Luca had a hard time concentrating. Seeing the obvious poverty of Freddie's family, Luca guessed that Freddie's short life had been harsh and difficult. He realized with a sadness he didn't fully understand that he really hadn't known Freddie. Just as he had never talked with Eli, he had never actually talked to Freddie.

Luca heard a sniffle and saw Madre wiping her eyes. He turned his attention to the service. The minister read Psalm 100:12: "So teach us to number our days, that we may apply our hearts unto wisdom."

As he was walking out of the church, the psalm was all Luca remembered. He went with Madre and shook hands with Freddie's family. Over to one side, he saw Creepy Eddie.

Luca walked over to where Eddie stood. "I'm sorry for the loss of your friend," Luca said. Then, wanting to say something else, he added, "I never got to know him." Luca extended his hand to Eddie.

Eddie shook Luca's hand. "Thank you, I'll sure miss him."

Luca looked up to see Missouri Compton watching him. He thought it was funny that she had gone to the funeral since he knew she would never have had anything to do with Freddie. It would be beneath her dignity.

Missouri walked over to him. "I've heard you were a hero," she said. She fluttered her eyes and looked down modestly.

"Not really," said Luca, although by now he had heard the same thing from several people.

"Well, you're my hero," said Missouri.

"I'm charmed," said Luca in a tone of voice that expressed his disdain. "But I don't want to be anybody's hero."

Missouri was taken aback. She forced a smile before turning to join a girlfriend who stood a little way off.

Madre rejoined Luca. "I'm going to the hospital," she said. "I can do more good there than here."

Right in front of everyone in the dispersing crowd, Luca gave his mother a hug. "See you at supper," he said.

Luca noticed that Madre's eyes had filled with tears again. But she forced a smile as she headed off toward the hospital.

Luca had no desire to follow the mourners to the cemetery. Instead, he headed toward Jim's house. He had crossed the street when he heard someone call out, "Hey, Luca!"

It was Jake Leighton. He bounded across the street to where Luca stood. "Some of the guys and I are going to play baseball a little later. Want to join us?"

"No thanks, I've promised to visit Jim this afternoon. Maybe we'll both join you sometime when he's better."

"Good. We'd like that. I'm off to the cemetery. Catch you later."

On the way to Jim's house, Luca realized he no longer cared about Missouri or Jake. A lot had changed in a few days. The infatuation with Missouri and his desire to join Jake's group seemed immature and stupid. How could he have ever thought that they were more interesting and important than Jim and Emmy?

Emmy was on the porch when Luca reached Jim's house. "I've heard you scared off a Yankee with one word." She wrinkled her nose. "You said your gun would make...macaroni...of the Yankee's chest?" She rolled her eyes.

Luca grinned. "Go away." He mimicked Jim's tone of voice and good-natured attempts to get Emmy to back off. "Just go away."

Author's Note

The main characters in **Anybody's Hero: The Battle of Old Men and Young Boys** are fictional. Yet the story turns on actual events that occurred in May and June of 1864. The battle fought on June 9, known as the Battle of Old Men and Young Boys, took place at Battery 27 on the Dimmock Line, at Petersburg, Virginia. The Petersburg Militia Reserves valiantly defended the city against overwhelming odds, holding off the Union forces until Confederate reinforcements arrived. I have tried to recreate as accurately as possible the circumstances of the battle, including details from the many accounts of what happened.

On June 15, 1864, the Union army attacked Petersburg again. In the next fifteen days, 16,569 men lost their lives at Petersburg. The city endured a ten-month siege before it fell to Union forces on April 3, 1865. The fall of Petersburg led directly to the end of the Confederacy. Ironically, if the citizens of Petersburg had not held off the Yankee attack on June 9 until reinforcements arrived, the terrible carnage of the last months of the Civil War might have been avoided.

Many of the buildings mentioned in the story— The Farmers Bank, the Courthouse, the Exchange Building, and the Trapezium House—can be seen today in Petersburg. The Exchange Building is called the Siege Museum, where a faceless doll named Pat is on display.

I have incorporated known facts about Petersburg whenever possible. A Mr. O'Hara built and owned the Trapezium House and Henry Clay Pate invented a revolving cannon that was built by the Petersburg firm of Tappey and Lumsden in 1861.

Glossary

Archer, Fletcher H. (1817–1902)

A veteran of the *Mexican War*, Major Archer commanded the *Militia Reserves* at the *Battle of Old Men and Young Boys*.

Battery

An area, sometimes raised, behind the earthworks, especially prepared for artillery. There were 55 batteries at intervals along the Dimmock Line.

Battle of New Orleans

A battle on January 8, 1815, in which Andrew Jackson decisively defeated the British in the *War of 1812*. Unknown to Jackson and the American army, the war had ended two weeks before the battle.

Battle of Old Men and Young Boys

A battle that took place on June 9, 1864, in which the citizens of Petersburg successfully defended their city from a massive Union attack.

Battle of Thermopylae

A battle in 480 B.C. where the Spartan King Leonidas and his 300 men died defending the narrow pass at Thermopylae against the vast army of the invading Persian general Xerxes during the Persian Wars. Their heroic sacrifice saved Greece from Persian domination.

bluecoats, bluebelly, bluebellies

Names Southerners called the *Union army* because they wore blue uniforms. The Union army soldiers were also known as *Federals* or Yankees.

City Point

A key staging area and supply depot for the Union army during the Petersburg Campaign, located where the Appomattox River flows into the James River.

Civil War (1861–1865)

The Civil War began when Southern states left or seceded from the Union and formed their own country, the Confederate States of America. The Northern states fought to preserve the Union while the South fought for its independence. Slavery was one of the issues that divided North and South. Southerners sometimes called it the *War of Secession.*

Confederacy

A short name for the Southern states that seceded from or left the United States and formed their own government called the Confederate States of America. The new country was called the Confederacy.

Confederate Army, Confederates

The armed forces of the South during the Civil War. Soldiers and sailors were called Confederates, Southerners, or *Rebels*.

Davis, Jefferson (1808–89)

President of the Confederate States of America from 1861–1865.

Dimmock Line

A horseshoe-shaped defensive line of fortifications constructed around Petersburg in 1862–1863. It was composed of earthworks and 55 batteries, spaced at intervals along the line.

Earthworks

An embankment made of earth and used for fortification.

Farmers Bank

Built in 1817, the Petersburg branch of Farmers Bank of Virginia is one of the oldest bank buildings in America.

Federals

One of the names the Southerners called the *Union army*.

Garibaldi, Giuseppe (1807–82)

An Italian patriot who in 1860 led 1,000 volunteers, called the "Red Shirts," in the conquest of Sicily and Naples. Sacrificing his republican ideas for the unification of Italy, he turned his conquests over to Victor Emmanuel II who became king of a united Italy.

kepi

A military cap with a circular top and visor.

lumbago

A painful condition of the lower back.

Mexican War (1846–48)

A war between the United States and Mexico. The immediate cause of the war was the American annexation of Texas.

Militia Reserves

Major Fletcher Archer organized the Militia Reserves. The Militia Reserves were called second class militia that was supposed to be composed of men aged 45 to 55 and boys aged 16 to 18. In fact, some of Archer's men were over 60 and under 16; one boy was 12.

minié ball

A civil war rifle bullet.

palaver

Idle talk.

Pat

A faceless doll in the Siege Museum in Petersburg. The doll was made by Martha Ann Davis on January 1, 1823, for Jane Powell Crawford, aged 21 months.

Pate, Henry Clay (dates unknown)

An inventor who developed the revolving cannon. Two models of the cannon were built in Petersburg by the firm of Tappey and Lumsden. One exploded, killing three men while it was being tested. The other can be seen in Petersburg, Virginia, at the Siege Museum.

Petersburg, Virginia

The key to capturing the Confederate capital at Richmond was taking the city of Petersburg, 30 miles away. With important roads and five railway lines, Petersburg was a key industrial center and the chief supply center for Richmond.

Trapezium House

A house in Petersburg at 244 North Market Street built in the shape of a trapezoid around 1817 by Charles O'Hara.

Union army

This was the army of the Northern states during the Civil War.

Voodoo

A religion that began in the Caribbean Islands. Its followers believe in spells, magic, and rituals.

War of 1812 (1812–1815)

A war between the United States and Great Britain over freedom of the seas.

War of Secession

Another name for the *Civil War*. This name was especially popular with Southerners.

Poem found inside Pat

On a Baby, which was made
for Miss Jane Powell Crawford
by her friend Martha Ann Davis
Cottage, January 1st, 1823—

Go harmless **Pat** and give delight
To little Jane from morn 'till night,
She'll press you fondly in her arms,
And think you have a thousand
            charms,
Sweetly she'll sing you by-ba-by—
While folded to her breast you lie,
Oft' times in gayest dress attir'd,
Prosperity will smile on thee,
And Jenny's idol you will be.
But I predict where e'er you go,
That various changes you will
            know,
And various *faces* you must wear,
If to sweet Jane, you would be dear.
Were you posses'd of feelings, I,
Should give to thee a parting sigh,
For many a rival you will have,
And Jane will oft' neglectful prove:
But surely thine's an envied state,
Unconscious en'en of *love* or *hate*,
Applause will never make you vain,
Or loss of *beauty* give you pain,
Adversity may frown on thee,
But still serene and calm you'll be,
Destined thro' various scenes to go,
A stranger to every woe.
A race unborn will gaze on thee
And think thou art a *prodigy*.

                    M.A.D.

Miss Jane P. Crawford was twenty-one months when this baby was made for her.
Courtesy of the Petersburg Museums, City of Petersburg, Va.

Resources

Bernard, George S. *War Talks of Confederate Veterans*. Petersburg, Va.: Fenn and Owen, 1892. Contains eyewitness accounts of the Battle of Old Men and Young Boys.

Henderson, William D. *Petersburg in the Civil War*. Lynchburg, Va.: H. E. Howard, Inc., 1998. This gives a good overview of Petersburg at the time of the Civil War.

Keiley, Anthony. *In Vinculis*. Petersburg, Va.: Daily Index, 1866. A lawyer's firsthand account of the events of June 9, 1864.

Robertson, William G. *The Battle of Old Men and Young Boys*. Lynchburg, Va.: H. E. Howard, Inc., 1989. This is the only complete historical study of the battle.

To Plan a Visit

Battle Site

Battery 27 no longer exists. A monument marks the site of the battle at the junction of US route 301 and South Boulevard in Petersburg, Virginia. The inscription now nearly obliterated by time and weather reads:

THE STONE MARKS THE SPOT WHERE THE OLD MEN AND BOYS OF PETERSBURG UNDER GEN. R.E. COLSTON AND COL. F.H. ARCHER 125 STRONG ON JUNE 9TH, 1864 DISTINGUISHED THEMSELVES IN A FIGHT WITH 1300 FEDERAL CAVALRY UNDER GEN. KAUTZ, GAINING TIME FOR THE DEFEAT OF THE EXPEDITION.

PLACED BY THE PETERSBURG CHAPTER U.D.C. MAY 1909.

Historic Petersburg, Virginia

A visit to the old town of Petersburg begins at the Visitor's Center on Old Towne Road. From here, you can walk to Courthouse Square, High Street, Farmers Bank, the Exchange Building, now the Siege

Monument marking the site of the Battle of Old Men and Young Boys, today just off US Route 301, Petersburg

Author's Photograph

Museum, and the Trapezium House. For more information contact:

Petersburg Visitor's Center, P.O. Box 2107, Petersburg, VA 23804

1-800-368-3595; http://www.petersburg-va.org

Pamplin Historical Park and
The National Museum of the Civil War Soldier

This museum complex consisting of a military encampment, the battlefield center, the National Museum of the Civil War Soldier, and Tudor Hall Plantation is devoted to the struggle for Petersburg in 1864–1865. For more information contact:

Pamplin Historical Park

6125 Boydton Plank Road

Petersburg, VA 23803

1-877-PAMPLIN; http://www.pamplinpark.org

Petersburg National Battlefield

There is a 37-mile driving tour of the battlefield. On the tour you can see the remains of the Dimmock Line and Confederate Batteries 5 and 9. For more information contact:

Superintendent, National Battlefield

1539 Hickory Hill Road

Petersburg, VA 23804

http://www.nps.gov/pete

" Well-researched historical fiction from heartrending to heart mending."

—Viky Pedigo, Rawls Byrd Elementary School

From the author of *Anybody's Hero!*

➤ Ten-year old Lottie is sold away from her mother at a slave auction and travels south tied to other slaves.

➤ The uncertainty of her future leads to an escape attempt, but morning finds the slave trader and his dogs closing in.

➤ This is the story of Lottie's struggle to overcome her fears and keep alive the hope that someday she will find her mother.

ISBN 1-57249-311-9   5-1/2" x 8-1/2"   PB $7.95

This historical novel is based on memoirs and other records describing the experiences of runaway slaves who found refuge at Fortress Monroe in Virginia during the Civil War. Life among the contraband slaves provides the setting for Lottie's story.

"Through scrupulous research, author Phyllis Hall Haislip has brought to light the little known story of hundreds of escaped slaves who received protection at the Union Army's Fortress Monroe in Virginia. In this gripping historical novel, Lottie and her older friend, Weza, escape a brutal slave trader and take refuge with Union soldiers. The period photos and drawings that illustrate the book provide important information about life in the fortress."

—*Washington Parent*

"Lottie's story offers a framework through which children can explore the issues of the Civil War, slavery, and human rights."

—*Civil War Book Review*

"Here is an exciting and unusual twist on the experiences of slaves who escaped from their owners during the Civil War. This 201 page paperback is greatly enhanced by old photographs, drawings, maps and songs that bring to life this period of American history for both teenagers and adult readers, who will share the terror and hope of ten-year-old Lottie in her quest for a new life. Highly recommended."

—African-American Cultural & Geanealogical Society of Illinois

"Although this is historical fiction, it provides a view of slave life, through the eyes of ten-year-old Lottie that is not well know. The pain of Lottie being separated and sold away from her mother is strongly felt as you read the author's account."

—*Children's Literature*

Though the words are over one hundred years old— their powerful stories still speak to us today.

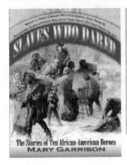

The Stories of Ten African-American Heroes
MARY GARRISON

> ➢ *Slavery impacted all age groups—this book paints a picture of what slave life was like for young people.*
>
> ➢ *Watch your father collapse after receiving one hundred lashes with a whip.*
>
> ➢ *Live in an attic for seven years to escape harassment.*
>
> ➢ *Risk your life escaping seven times from seven different owners.*
>
> ➢ *Be brutally beaten and scarred at age nine.*

ISBN 1-57249-272-4   8-1/4" x 10-1/4"   HC $19.95

This book portrays everyday life of enslaved children and families (meals, food, clothing, education, Christmas customs, etc.). It also exposes young readers to true stories (based on over one hundred-year-old firsthand narratives) of former slaves, providing a deeper understanding of the impact of slavery on individuals. These stories illustrate how men, women, and children of character made contributions despite their hardships.

Students who read this book will have a clearer understanding of the daily life of a slave, and what slavery did to the lives and dreams of individual people. It provides the understanding for young readers that today's freedoms are based on building blocks from the past.

"Drawing directly on the narratives of 10 men and women who escaped slavery, this stirring collective biography brings their history very close....Garrison does a great job of weaving into each narrative many actual quotes, illustrations such as historical prints and facsimiles, and the drama of how and where the stories were recorded." —*ALA Booklist*

"This is a solid, illustrated work and one that will enhance young readers' understanding of slavery and those who struggled against its bonds."
—*Children's Literature*

"Although *Slaves Who Dared* is intended for kids ages 10 and up, the book is important for all ages. It uncovers a whole new picture of the Civil War era and introduces readers to people not often heard or highlighted....Readers are able to put a brave face with a courageous life story and recognize the true meaning of the word *hero*." —*Civil War Book Review*

"Your story made me feel like I was in the story. You will be at the top of my authors list!" —*Kelsey Stout, age 11, Hendersonville, N.C.*